'Oh, come on,
the innocent w

Kane's voice was a
too well for that. All these sudden observations
on life? This sexy little body when before you
never seemed to care one way or another what
you looked like? There's a man in your life,
isn't there? My sweet assistant, the one woman
in life I always felt I could trust, has found
herself a lover.'

Dear Reader

This month, I would like to ask you to think about the kind of heroine you would like to find in our stories. Do you think she should be sweet and gentle, on the look-out for a man who will be able to care for and nurture her, or should the heroine be able to give as good as she gets, throwing punch for punch, and quite capable of standing up for herself? If you have any opinions on this matter please let us know, so that we can continue to give you the books you want to read!

The Editor

Cathy Williams is Trinidadian and was brought up on the twin islands of Trinidad and Tobago. She was awarded a scholarship to study in Britain, and came to Exeter University in 1975 to continue her studies into the great loves of her life: languages and literature. It was there that Cathy met her husband, Richard. Since they married, Cathy has lived in England, originally in the Thames Valley but now in the Midlands. Cathy and Richard have one child, a daughter, Charlotte.

Recent titles by the same author:

CHARADE OF THE HEART
NAIVE AWAKENING
TOO SCARED TO LOVE

BITTERSWEET LOVE

BY

CATHY WILLIAMS

MILLS & BOON LIMITED
ETON HOUSE, 18-24 PARADISE ROAD
RICHMOND, SURREY TW9 1SR

First published in Great Britain 1993
by Mills & Boon Limited

© Cathy Williams 1993

Australian copyright 1993
Philippine copyright 1993
This edition 1993

ISBN 0 263 78178 X

Set in Times Roman 10 on 12 pt.
01-9308-53371 C

Made and printed in Great Britain

CHAPTER ONE

NATALIE could feel the spring in her step become heavier
and heavier the closer she got to the awesome glass edifice
that housed the Marshall Corporation.

Why not admit it? she told herself. I don't want to
see Kane Marshall. I don't want to see his face, I don't
want to hear his voice, I don't want to feel that awful,
sickening rollercoaster of emotions every time he glances
in my direction.

Not that he had the slightest idea what went on underneath that bright, efficient smile of hers. If he had, she
would have left his employment immediately.

She stuck her hands into her jacket pocket and stood
still for a moment outside the building, letting the cool
summer breeze whip her hair across her face, glaring at
the squares of glass, already hating him for what he did
to her.

She was twenty-seven years old, and she had spent the
last five of those years hopelessly in love with a man
who wouldn't have noticed her if she had stood naked
on top of his desk with a rose between her teeth.

He was the boss, and she was his personal assistant.
He discussed work with her, trusted her completely in
that respect. In fact, he had jokingly told her once before
that the office would seize up should she ever decide to
take her talents elsewhere. She had smiled politely at the
compliment, wondering how it was that some compliments could sound very much like insults.

But she knew how he saw her. Plain, slightly over-weight, owlish behind her spectacles, brimming over with crisp efficiency. Neat navy suits and sensible shoes. Reliable little Natalie Robins.

Even when, six month ago, he had taken her out to dinner, and announced that he would be leaving the country to set up a new and important subsidiary in the Far East, he had had no qualms in handing her the reins of responsibility. He would be accessible by telephone and on the fax machine. The rest he was quite confident that she could handle.

Six months without being subjected to the force of his aggressive, dominant personality, was a long time. Long enough to think very carefully indeed about where her life was going. Long enough to lose quite a bit of weight, to get rid of those awful spectacles that did nothing for her eyes, to style her hair into something more resembling a tousled mane than the lank bun which she had been wont to wear to work every day.

Long enough to make up her mind once and for all that loving Kane Marshall was a disease which she would overcome if she died in the process.

Even so, standing here in front of the building and knowing that she would be seeing him for the first time in six months made her skin prickle with alarm. She was realistic enough to realise that her idiotic love for him was responsible for that clutching knot in the pit of her stomach, but that didn't mean that she had to like it.

She took a deep breath and quickly covered the ground towards the building, her feet automatically taking her to the private lift which would carry her straight up to his office. The knot in her stomach seemed to have grown, making it difficult for her to breathe, and her hands were balled into nervous fists in her pockets.

Thank heavens her cool, slightly aloof face betrayed none of this inner turmoil. The outward package might have undergone a few renovations here and there, but basically she was the same collected person as she always had been. She had spent years perfecting the ability to express on her face only what she wanted the world to see, and as she stepped into the office now, quietly hanging her jacket on the coat-stand next to her large L-shaped desk, she thanked God for that.

She knocked perfunctorily and pushed open the connecting door between her outer office and Kane's main one, unable to prevent her quick intake of breath as her eyes rested on his tall, powerful frame. He was standing half turned from her, staring out of the window, his thoughts miles away. He couldn't have heard her soft knock.

She had thought her memory to be quite vivid, but now, seeing him for the first time in months, he seemed so much more overpowering than she had remembered. The black, springy hair was slightly shorter than when he had left, his frame a little leaner, as though he had spent a great deal of time working out. Or maybe it was simply that his tan created that illusion, because he was certainly more bronzed now than she could ever remember him being.

'It's good to have you back, Mr Marshall,' Natalie forced herself to speak into the silence, afraid that she would be unable to tear her eyes away from him until he turned around and caught her in the act of watching him.

He turned to face her, and whatever he had been about to say remained unspoken as his eyes swept over her. She could see the surprise written there, and she met his gaze blankly, steeling herself for the inevitable sarcasm.

'Natalie?' he finally asked, moving towards her, his hands in his pockets. He circled her, his green eyes amused as he inspected her with the thoroughness of a racehorse owner inspecting a horse. 'You've changed.' He continued to look at her, his brilliant eyes missing nothing, and she had the intensely uncomfortable feeling that she was being leisurely stripped by someone who was quite an expert at the procedure.

'People tend to,' Natalie said crisply, moving away from him and positioning herself closer to the door. 'From time to time.'

'Do they?' He sounded as though this was a novel concept, but she could still see the amusement lurking there in the depths of his eyes and it irritated her. She had forgotten just how quickly he could get under her skin. 'I haven't,' he pointed out, returning to his desk and gesturing for her to sit in the chair facing his.

'You look much browner,' Natalie said non-committally. 'Was it very hot out there?'

'Oh, very. And what was the weather like over here? Do tell.' He leaned back and surveyed her from under his thick black lashes, his eyes flicking once again over her body, resting on the gentle swell of her breasts, which she had hitherto played down under muted, baggy clothes, as if he couldn't quite get to grips with the transformation.

'I'm merely trying to make small talk,' Natalie said, frowning.

'Don't you think we've known each other too long for small talk?'

It was the sort of remark that, in different circumstances, might well have sounded quite intimate, but here, in the clinical severity of his office, she knew what he meant. They had worked together for so long that they operated with the kind of familiarity that came to old, married couples.

'Besides,' he was saying, moving on from his offhand observation, 'if we're going to play that game, let's at least talk about something slightly more interesting. Like what the hell has happened to you?'

'Not a great deal,' Natalie informed him, deliberately misunderstanding his question. 'I've taken up squash and swimming. My sister has made me godmother to her little boy. And, of course, I've pretty much kept on top of the workload, you'll be pleased to hear, although, as you suspected, that Grafton deal is proving trickier than was originally anticipated. But I discussed all that on the telephone with you a couple of days ago. The file is on my desk, if you'd care to see it.'

She rose to get it, too nervously conscious of his eyes on her to remain in the room any longer.

'Sit down,' he barked. 'I haven't laid eyes on you for six months, dammit, to find that you've gone and got yourself overhauled. You haven't found yourself a man, by any chance, have you?' There was a thread of suspicion in his voice.

Natalie gave him a look that would freeze water, and he laughed.

'Good. I can't afford to have you besotted with any man. There's too much work on here at the moment for that little luxury. The Hong Kong operation is going to have a massive knock-on effect on our outlets over here.'

He began rooting through some paperwork on his desk and she glared at the downturned dark head. She had become quite accustomed to this trait of his. He would pick up a topic, explore it for a while, like a child with a plaything, and then when he was satisfied that there was nothing left to discover about it, or when it began to bore him, he would drop it without a backward glance.

It was how he treated the women in his life, and there were enough of them. Blonde, brunette, red-haired, all perfectly proportioned Barbie doll look-alikes who adorned his arm for just as long as he wanted them to, before boredom set in.

It never failed to amaze her that she had fallen in love with someone whose character she was quite capable of assassinating with a few easy strokes. How could anyone with a scrap of common sense actually love a man whose idea of involvement was a diamond necklace and a weekend in Rome, work permitting, and whose attitude to parting was a philosophical shrug of the shoulders?

Now, she thought acidly, he had sized up her transformation, made sure that it would not cause any ripples in her work life, and, that done, was quite content to get back to the business in hand.

For once, though, Natalie was not going to accept his change of direction with equanimity. Maybe six months of freedom from his engulfing, mesmeric personality had taken their toll in more ways than one after all.

She looked at him, her grey eyes level, and said coolly, 'You can rest assured that the presence of a man in my life would not affect my work here in the slightest.'

He glanced up from what he was doing, his black brows drawn together in a frown.

'But there is no man, is there?' He looked at her doubtfully, and she could read what was going through his head.

Natalie Robins, prior to reconstruction, plump, unappealing, was safe and reliable. Now he wasn't too sure. She had moved on from that image and there was the niggling suspicion that men might actually begin to feature on the scene.

She smiled expressionlessly at him. 'And if there were? Do the hordes of women in your life interfere with your ability to work?'

He sat back in the chair and clasped his hands behind his head, his green eyes giving her their full attention. There was interest in his face, as though the nature of her question had startled him slightly, but not enough to deter him from responding.

'Nothing interferes with my ability to work. You, of all people should know that.'

'Then why should you assume that it would be any different for me?'

'Women are a part of my life,' he said bluntly, his green eyes roving over her face. Then he leaned back and stared at her from under those thick black eyelashes. 'I know how to handle them. I can put them into perspective.'

There was no need for him to say anything further. Natalie knew well enough what he was getting at. The unspoken implication was that she had no experience with men, so how could she possibly handle something as extraordinary as a love-affair?

She looked at him coldly and when she spoke her voice was well modulated and perfectly controlled, even though inside she was bristling with anger.

'Can't you just?' She lowered her eyes and began flicking through her typing pad.

'And what exactly does that remark mean?' He circled round his desk to perch on the edge of it in front of her, and she wondered whether this was as casual as it appeared to be. She wouldn't put it past him to subconsciously use body language like that to addle her.

'It means that your treatment of women, from what I've seen, leaves a great deal to be desired.' She stared straight ahead of her, her profile neat and clean.

'Well, thank you for that remarkable piece of insight into my love life.' His voice was still threaded with amusement. 'I had no idea that you disapproved so strongly of it. Or maybe I had.' He rubbed his chin thoughtfully and Natalie gritted her teeth together because she knew that he was laughing at her. 'Yes,' he continued slowly, 'your disapproval was always there in that tight expression you wore every time a woman walked through the door. But you never actually came right out and said anything. Perhaps your new body image has brought on a change of personality?' The question hung in the air, and Natalie sincerely hoped that he didn't expect any answer, because she had no intention of providing one.

'Well?' he pressed. 'Has it? I hope not. I liked you the way you were. My life's too complicated without you suddenly deciding that you need to discover yourself.'

'In that case,' she said calmly, 'I'll make sure that I discover myself outside working hours.'

What an arrogant, selfish swine, she thought. How could I have ever fallen in love with you?

She thought that they had killed the subject. What else was there to say?

His movement when he leaned over to twirl one long strand of hair between his finger surprised her so much that her body jerked around and she faced him angrily. He laughed, his eyes mocking, and folded his arms.

'I still can't get over this transformation,' he murmured. 'What prompted it? If it wasn't a man, then what?'

Natalie stood up, working on the theory that she would feel far less disadvantaged if she was at least on eye level with him, and then instantly regretted it because that brought her far too close to his dark, handsome face.

Was it really any wonder that women found him so irresistible? Even with all her defences in full working order Natalie could feel that intangible pull he exerted over the opposite sex. He had that particularly lazy, self-assured brand of sexuality that could conquer without a great deal of effort. She had seen even the most hardened of feminists fall victim to it, and every time she saw it, it made her annoyed. It just didn't seem fair that one man should be so shamelessly magnetic.

'That,' she said frozenly, 'has to be the most chauvinistic remark I have ever heard.'

He laughed. 'Really? That just goes to show how little experience you have of the opposite sex.'

She looked away quickly to hide the faint flush that had crept up her cheeks. God only knew why she had allowed this sort of personal conversation to sneak up on her and catch her unawares. It never usually happened.

'Well,' she bit out defensively, 'if you are anything to go by, then I'm heartily glad about that.'

She looked at him, horrified by what she had just said.

'Are you?' His eyes were curious, and she realised that her remark, rather than ending their conversation, had had just the opposite effect.

'I am, as a matter of fact,' she muttered under her breath. She could hear her heart hammering away in her chest, and would have given anything to have been able to sit back down, but if she did that might delude him into thinking that she was actually interested in this conversation.

'I'm mortally offended,' he said, his eyes gleaming with suppressed amusement, and she could have hit him. What a keen sense of humour. Was this his idea of getting back into the routine? By starting off the morning with a little laugh at her expense?

'Mortally?' she said, refusing to share the joke. 'In that case, I'll try and make time to come to the funeral.'

He laughed and threw her an appreciative look.

'I can't tell you how nice it is to be back here, at the mercy of that vicious tongue of yours. The secretary I had out there was awful. She spent six months complaining and generally acting as though working for me was on a par with enforced labour. If she hadn't come with a personal recommendation, I would have got rid of her so fast she wouldn't have known what had hit her. But I didn't want to offend my man over there, so I stuck it out. Just.'

He moved back to his chair and Natalie released a sigh of relief.

Poor girl, she thought sympathetically. She could have understood the reaction. Kane Marshall could be very intimidating at times. When it came to work, he could be unforgiving, and his peculiar ability to grasp complex matters quickly made him short-tempered and impatient with anything he saw as ignorance.

These were not lovable traits—not that Kane would see it that way.

He began rattling instructions to her and her private thoughts were quickly swamped under a torrent of shorthand and paperwork. He showed her pictures of the new complex and Natalie watched in appreciation, asking sensible questions, fully relaxed now that they were both involved in work and nothing more. They began going over some reports, and she expertly flicked through them to the relevant spots, rapidly jotting down amendments in the margins as Kane went through them with her.

It was midday when she next glanced at her watch and she looked up at him to find him staring at her with an intensity that confused her for a split second, before she had time to gather her thoughts together.

They had been sitting close to one another, the reports between them. Now she moved her chair away just a fraction, and as surreptitiously as she could so that he would not notice.

'You look completely different without your glasses,' he remarked musingly. 'I never noticed what a peculiar shade your eyes were. Pure, undiluted grey.' His voice was light, but his expression was disturbingly serious.

Natalie blinked, taken aback. For once, her talent for repartee deserted her, and she stammered, 'Is—is that a compliment? If it is, thank you. But what about those figures we were talking about?' Her fingers were trembling very slightly, and she shoved them on to her lap in irritation.

Couldn't she trust herself not to react like this after all this time? Shaking hands because he happened to make a personal comment on her appearance, schoolgirl blushes because his eyes on her face betrayed the vaguest element of interest which she had never noticed being there before.

It was ridiculous, pathetic. She refused to be either ridiculous or pathetic.

'Why don't we discuss it over lunch?' he said smoothly, standing up and raking his fingers through his hair, his eyes already off her as he prowled into his office for his jacket. 'We can go to that wine bar,' he threw over his shoulder, 'you know the one. If it's still there. I had no idea how much could change in six short months, until I saw you.'

He re-emerged into the room and frowned when he saw that she was still sitting at her desk, stacking some of the files in order, skimming through the paperwork that would need actioning when she returned from lunch.

'I can't go,' Natalie informed him flatly, and she didn't think he could have been more surprised if she had told him that she was about to become a belly-dancer in Egypt.

'You can't go?'

Natalie didn't look up. 'That's right. I've started working out at a gym near by during my lunch hours.'

He paced across the room to where she was sitting and she reluctantly met his eyes.

'You can skip today's session, in that case,' he said in that tone of voice which she had come to recognise over the years. It was the one he used when he was not about to take no for an answer.

'I'm sorry,' Natalie informed him politely. 'I've arranged to meet a friend there; we're going to grab a salad afterwards.'

She switched off the computer terminal and reached underneath for the bag which she kept under the desk and which contained her spare case of make-up and a towel, as well as her keep-fit gear. Kane continued to watch her as though she had suddenly taken leave of her senses, and it made her want to laugh.

Except the laughter would have been streaked with self-disgust. Had love made her so amenable to him that she had always been willing to bend to whatever he wanted? From the expression on his face, it certainly seemed so.

'So you have changed more than simply the pack-aging,' he said with a hard, assessing smile. 'You've suddenly turned into Miss Popular of the Year. What a revelation.'

Natalie's fingers tightened on her holdall. She knew what lay behind that biting cynicism in his voice. He had become accustomed to her readiness to comply with everything he wanted. Her work had been the main-spring of her existence. Everything else fell around it and somehow slotted in. Now it was different. From here on in she intended to live her life to the fullest, and work would simply have to slot itself in. She wouldn't slack off, but on the other hand she would no longer allow it to absorb her the way it had done. That was one of the things she had decided in his absence and she intended to stick to it.

In the past, she had been like an addict, feeding on her blind love for him, open to exploitation. No more. And the sooner he realised that, the better.

'If there are things to discuss outside working time,' she said, ignoring his gibe and bypassing him to the door, 'I'm more than happy to work overtime tonight. But I shall have to leave by seven, I'm afraid. I'm going out.'

He followed her out of the office and into the lift as it silently transported them to the foyer.

'Where?'

This was getting on his nerves, she could sense that. Kane was someone who liked being in control—in fact he saw it as his prerogative. The fact that she had altered in his absence to someone whom he didn't know and could no longer control irked him.

'That's none of your business,' Natalie murmured sweetly, flashing him a smile which made him scowl.

They were outside the building now and she glanced across at him, her breath catching in her throat as his sexual allure engulfed her.

That, she thought, was one thing that hadn't changed. Unfortunately. The glare from the sun, which normally was so relentless in emphasising the inadequacies of people's features, threw his into relief and somehow made them more startling. What, under the synthetic lights in an office, were angular and impressive, in daylight were devastatingly sexy.

'I'll see you after lunch,' she said firmly.

'And make sure you're back on time,' he responded in a silky voice, which had just the smallest element of warning in it. 'All these frantic activities are one thing, just so long as they don't interfere with your working life.'

Natalie glared at him, the smile dropping from her face.

'That's not fair! I've never shirked my responsibilities, you know that!'

'I never suggested that you had.'

'Then why are you implying that I'm suddenly going to start now?'

He looked down at her, a small smile twisting his lips although his green eyes were hard and calculating.

'For reasons that I can't begin to fathom, you've decided to change your image. And very successful you've been too. But I think it's only fair to warn you that I won't be lenient when it comes to making allowances for your suddenly booming social life.' He shot her a calculating look. 'And love life, for that matter. Burning the candle at both ends isn't going to win any Brownie points with me.'

'I'll bear that in mind,' Natalie said stiffly. And thanks so much for the warm welcome, she thought to herself. 'I'll see you after lunch,' she repeated, 'and you needn't worry that I won't be back on time.'

He had the grace to flush slightly at her tone of voice but Natalie was in no mood to relent. Kane Marshall was a trying man to work for at the best of times. He was demanding, rarely voluble in his gratitude when she had worked longer and harder than was usual, and she had never once abused his silent assumption that her dedication to his company was paramount.

How dare he stand there and inform her that he would now be keeping an eye on her to make sure that she kept to his rigidly imposed schedule?

She turned away and walked quickly in the direction of the gym. It was a couple of stops on the Underground from the office, but by foot it was no distance at all and she had become accustomed to grabbing as much exercise as she could.

As she walked quickly along, she was aware of the odd appreciative glance in her direction and she couldn't prevent a grin from forming. Poor Kane. What a shock. There was a certain delicious enjoyment to be had from the thought that, amused as he was by her change of appearance, there was just the tiniest element of pique that she had had the temerity to do it all without first consulting him.

The smile stayed on her face all through her lunch-hour and she was still wearing it when she returned to the office just before one-thirty.

Kane was at his desk, poring over a pile of reports, a half-finished sandwich next to him, and she was moving towards her own desk, a grin on her face, when he said through the opened door, 'I see you enjoyed yourself.'

Natalie stopped in her tracks and looked at him, her grin still lingering on her face.

'Yes, thank you.' She went to stick her bag under the desk and he called out to her,

'Good for you. I wouldn't want to impose on your post-work-out euphoria, but could you see your way to fetching me a cup of coffee? And there are a few questions I'd like to ask on that Wilkes project.'

The grin faded and she glared at the wall between them. He was spoiling for a fight. She could hear it in his tone of voice and she could see it in that lazy pose he adopted when she walked into his office a few minutes later with a mug of coffee. Hands clasped behind his head, eyes narrowed on her. Only a complete idiot would be fooled into thinking that he was relaxed.

She carefully placed the coffee in front of him and sat down.

'The Wilkes project?' she reminded him, fixing him with a glassy, encouraging smile.

Funny to think that she had missed all this restless aggression. How could she have forgotten exactly how uncomfortable he was capable of making her feel?

'Ah, yes,' he said smoothly, 'the Wilkes project. It needed a few bits and pieces tying up when I left the country six months ago. I see from the file that the bits and pieces are still waiting to be tied up. Problems there or just lack of interest?' Natalie gave a barely audible sigh and he said in a very soft, very cutting voice, 'Dear me. I do hope I'm not boring you.'

Count to ten, she thought. Remember that old saying about patience being a virtue, because right now she needed a huge supply of it to cope with Kane in one of these determined-to-needle moods. His nose had temporarily been thrown out of joint and he wasn't about to let her forget that in a hurry.

'Not at all,' Natalie replied calmly. 'I was going to explain what's happened on that to you anyway.'

'Were you? Then explain on.'

'We delivered a shipment of sub-standard goods to them and they've been waiting for a rather large credit for the past two months.'

His black brows flew upwards. 'Two months? And who the hell is handling that account?'

Natalie told him and then watched as he roared his anger down the line. Two months' problems cleared up in a two-minute phone call. No humming and hedging with Kane Marshall. She sat in silence as he got Ben Wilkes on the line, turned on the charm that had helped to make him the powerful businessman that he was, and listened as he not only wrapped up their deal but managed to persuade them to buy far more than they had originally intended to.

When he replaced the receiver he shot her a smile of genuine amusement. The sort of smile that reminded her with sickening force precisely why she had learned to cultivate her implacable exterior—because smiles like that were made to kill.

'Business,' he said lazily, 'can be so easy, if you know how.'

'Those credits were taking rather a long time to be resolved,' she admitted.

'People should realise that timidity and short-sighted penny-pinching doesn't go a long way to making money.'

'Not everyone puts making money at the top of their list of priorities, though,' Natalie said under her breath, and he leant towards her, his black brows meeting in a frown.

'Where the hell are you getting these ideas from? Of course making money is important. Ambition is the fuel that drives us on.'

Natalie hesitated, wondering whether she should take the side of discretion, and then on impulse she threw caution to the winds and said with heartfelt sincerity, 'You mean ambition is the fuel that drives *you* on. Some people might find it just a little bit too tiring.'

'Some people?' He stared at her shrewdly. 'Some people or one in particular?'

'What are you talking about?' Natalie asked, confused.

'Oh, come on, Natalie,' he drawled, 'don't play the innocent with me. We know each other too well for that. All these sudden observations on life? This sexy little body when before you never seemed to care one way or another what you looked like? There's a man in your life, isn't there?' He leaned closer towards her, his sharp brown features drawn in lines of interested amusement. 'Don't try and tell me there isn't. My sweet assistant, the one woman in life I always felt I could trust, has found herself a lover. I can almost smell it on you.'

Anger drained her face of colour then sent it flooding back into her cheeks. She stood up and without thinking slapped him across the face. Hard. She could feel her hand stinging from the impact and watched in horror as his face reddened from the force of her slap.

'I'm sorry,' she said weakly, her eyes wide. 'I don't know what came over me.'

His eyes were not so amused now. In fact, they were glinting with fury. He leaned over, one hand on his desk, and with the other he pulled her towards him, dislodging the clips in her hair so that it spilled over her face and shoulders.

'Don't you ever do that again; is that clear?'

Their eyes met and for the briefest of moments she felt as though she would swoon from the sheer, over-powering nearness of him, then she tightened her mouth in a firm line.

'You provoked me,' she said, knowing that she would be far wiser not to prolong the situation, but unable to relinquish the bit from between her teeth.

'I pay you to work for me. I don't need to cope with your temper tantrums.'

Natalie's mouth dropped open in amazement. Her temper tantrums? How dared he stand there and act as though she had manoeuvred the whole thing? As though she were some bubble-headed female throwing a fit for no reason?

She bit back the torrent of heated arguments on the tip of her tongue, and said tightly, 'Of course. Sir. I'll try not to forget it.'

It didn't seem such a good idea to add another sarcastic 'Sir' at the end of her reply, much as she would have liked to.

'Good.' His face was still only inches away from hers, his hand in her hair, half hidden under the jumbled mass. 'I have a meeting to go to now. It should last the remainder of the day. I hope that tomorrow you will be back to your normal self.'

He released her abruptly and turned away and Natalie glared at his back.

'I take it,' she said as he strode out of the office, her composure once more firmly back in place, 'that you don't need me to work overtime this evening?'

He turned to face her with an unreadable expression.

'No,' he said abruptly, 'not this evening. As a matter of fact, I have made some arrangements that are rather more stimulating than work.'

As he left the room, Natalie wandered to her desk and sat down heavily. She felt as though she had been through a wringer, and his parting words left her cold with dismay and a certain impotent anger that was directed against herself.

Because she knew where he was going. Maison Française. Chic, expensive, fine food and wine. His favourite haunt when it came to entertaining members of the opposite sex.

The only thing she didn't know was whom he would be going with. It certainly wouldn't be his dear old grandma.

But most of all she didn't want to care and she did.

Well, she was going to let that ruin her life, was she? Let him begin his round of seductions with that endless queue of women patiently waiting to get their hands on him.

Just so long as he never realised that she was in that queue as well.

CHAPTER TWO

LATER that evening, as Natalie dressed for her evening out, she couldn't help thinking with bewildered frustration that the cycle of emotions which she had sworn would be harnessed had managed quite successfully to survive Kane's six-month absence, and was now rearing its ugly head once again. Like a beast that had temporarily hibernated, but was already wakening, slowly stretching and testing the water.

She carefully applied her eye-shadow and glared at the reflection staring back at her. What was the good of even thinking about the wretched man? It had seemed so easy, when he wasn't around, to let thoughts of him slide to the background. He had been a constant background presence which she could handle without too much difficulty.

Now, in the space of just one day, he had filled the office with his overpowering personality and all her well-controlled thoughts had been shot to hell.

Great company I'm going to be tonight, she thought with a grimace. A regular barrel of laughs.

She had arranged to meet her friend Claire and Claire's brother at a restaurant near Covent Garden, a new place which specialised in Swiss food. Personally, she couldn't think what food the Swiss had to call their own, but she was game.

She had known Claire since she was a teenager and the company would be good. Eric, from what she vaguely remembered when she had last met him years ago, was good fun, and after the tension of today it would probably be just what the doctor ordered.

They were waiting for her when she arrived at the restaurant one hour later.

Natalie looked around her briefly, scanning the place with interest. It was small, tastefully decorated in cool creams and pinks, and had the eager atmosphere of somewhere very new and still keen to impress. Not that she could see much need for that, since the place was already quite busy, most of the tables taken with a selection of well-dressed women and their similiarly well-dressed counterparts. It was all very muted and in terribly good taste, but pleasing nevertheless. Natalie looked across to her friend and waved, hurrying across to their table.

Claire was a petite redhead, bubbly and vivacious, and her brother, whom Natalie recalled as work-shy and good-natured, had, she discovered with wry amusement, become a qualified accountant and was now deeply conservative.

'I never thought I'd see you in a navy blue suit, Eric,' she said with a smile, when Claire had excused herself to go to the ladies' room. 'In fact, I never thought I'd see you in a suit at all. What's the world coming to when you can't rely on people not to remain the same?'

They laughed and he parried with a few remarks of his own on how much she had changed, his eyes informing her that he appreciated the changes. He was comfortable company. Amusing, intelligent and undemanding. Natalie was in exactly the right mood for undemanding company. It relaxed her and she felt as though she needed relaxing.

She was leaning forward, laughing at something he had said, when a familiar deep voice spoke from behind her.

'What a surprise. I had no idea this sort of place was your cup of tea.'

Natalie swivelled around and watched in alarm as Kane moved around to face her. What on earth was he doing here? He wasn't going to stay and chat, was he? She sincerely hoped not.

Her eyes slid across to his companion, a tall blonde with an amazing figure. Natalie recognised her instantly. She had been seeing Kane before he left for the Far East. From the way she was clinging to his arm, it was obvious that his six-month absence had done nothing to staunch her ardour. Her name was Anna, and in the past she had barely managed to mutter a few words to Natalie, never mind glance in her direction. Now, however, her emerald-green eyes were narrowed into slits.

'Are you the same girl who worked for Kane?' she asked, without the slightest hint of embarrassment. 'Robin something? Or was it something Robin?' She laughed but her eyes remained hard and assessing.

Natalie looked at her calmly. 'Yes, I am.'

Anna threw her a look of stunned disbelief, and then issued a sharp smile to Claire, who was surveying the interchange with interest, and to Eric who was rather more embarrassed than interested.

'Hasn't she changed?'

'Hasn't she,' Natalie replied drily, sparing her friends the necessity of trying to find a response to that one.

'Natalie's been on some kind of health kick in my absence,' Kane interjected, his eyes resting on her face with the merest shadow of accusation. He looked across to Eric and raised one eyebrow imperceptibly, just enough

for Natalie to realise what he was thinking. She ignored
the questioning gleam in his eyes and plastered a blank
smile on her face.

'Has she?' Anna exclaimed. She nestled against Kane
possessively.

What does he see in them? Natalie asked herself with
a sharp pang of jealousy. Stupid question. Their bodies
of course. Kane had all the mental stimulation he could
handle at work. Every woman he had ever been out with,
and there had been no shortage of them over the years,
had been a physical work of art. Leggy, seductive.
Everything I'm not, Natalie admitted with honesty. Even
with my new improved shape and daring hairstyle I'll
never have that sort of feline, vampish grace that at-
tracts him.

She gave Eric a warm smile, a subconscious desire to
remind Kane and herself that he wasn't the only man in
the world, and he looked momentarily dazzled.

'I've often wanted to go on a health kick,' Anna was
saying with a flirtatious smile that expertly managed to
include both men and neither of the women. 'Of course,
I haven't got the incentive that you had.' She addressed
her observation to Natalie. 'When you're overweight it's
so much more motivating to do that sort of thing, isn't
it?'

'Isn't it?' Natalie agreed politely. She gave Kane a look
that said, Is this the best you could come up with for a
date? and his lips thinned.

'Shall we go to our table, darling?' he murmured to
Anna, and she gave a throaty laugh of assent.

Natalie watched as they walked across to a table in
the far corner of the room. The best table, naturally.
Kane had only to show himself at a restaurant and the
waiters would appear from nowhere, madly dashing

around him, as if sensing his unspoken authority and responding to it.

When she had first joined the company, Natalie had been impressed by this reaction. Now it irritated her. He was just a man, after all. Couldn't they see that? If the rest of the world treated Kane like a normal human being, instead of a demi-god, then he might just get it into that head of his that he wasn't a cut above everyone else. Not that he ever intimated as much, but that easy self-confidence and lazy assurance spoke volumes.

Across the room she could see him looking absolutely absorbed in whatever Anna was saying. Maybe they were planning what they would get up to after their three-course meal was out of the way. After all, Natalie thought acidly, they had some catching up to do, and she doubted very much of it involved conversation.

For the remainder of the evening, she found her attention drifting off towards Kane and Anna, speculating on all sorts of things, compulsively reading Anna's body language as she leaned towards Kane, giving him a bird's-eye view of the shadowy valley between her breasts, and twirling the long stem of her wine glass.

It was a relief when they rose to leave, Kane nodding briefly in her direction as he ushered Anna towards the door, with the usual subservient head waiter in attendance, like a fussy mother hen.

'Good-looking man, your boss,' Claire said, following Natalie's eyes.

'I suppose so.' She shrugged and concentrated on her cup of coffee and the tempting little dish of *petits fours* which she was having trouble resisting.

'Was that his wife?'

'Wife?' Natalie snorted expressively. 'I think he considers marriage as one of those odd things that other people get up to in their spare time.'

'And you don't?' Eric asked softly, his pale blue eyes looking at her curiously.

Natalie flushed and didn't say anything.

'I think marriage is terribly important,' he continued in the same speculative voice, 'but without the emotion involved. A business agreement, so to speak.'

Natalie looked at him, surprised, and out of the corner of her eye she saw Claire shake her head, warning her off the inevitable response.

Later, as she was about to step into the taxi to go home, Eric pulled her to one side and asked in an undertone how she felt about seeing him again.

'It seems a shame to vanish out of each other's lives for another six years,' he said with a little laugh, and she agreed.

'I'd love to see you again,' she responded warmly, 'just so long as we get one thing straight. No emotional ties, no involvement.'

Eric nodded. 'Same here,' he muttered with heartfelt intensity.

She gave him her phone number, rattling it off in a rush as the taxi driver eyed her with ill-concealed impatience, barely concerned whether he got in touch with her again or not. People, she noticed, had a habit of making showy gestures which rarely got followed up. Anyway, however nice Eric was, he could only end up being a complication in her life, and the less of those she had, the better.

She promptly relegated the entire incident to the back of her mind and forgot about it. That was the one thing to be said for working for Kane Marshall. It was impossible to concentrate on anything else when he was around. He was a sure-fire cure for most problems, because the minute she stepped foot into the office she immediately forgot about them all.

He was already there when she arrived there the following morning. He had loosened his tie and the sleeves of his white silk shirt were rolled to the elbows. He looked as though he had been hard at it for hours, even though it was still only eight-thirty in the morning.

'Good morning,' Natalie said, hanging up her lightweight jacket and automatically pouring them both a cup of coffee. Her huge grey eyes were level and serene, but inside her head a thousand thoughts were seething. Where had he and Anna gone after the restaurant? Had they made love? The thought pierced through her and she firmly pursed her lips together just in case some unwary moan escaped.

All these years, watching him from the sidelines, knowing that he slept with those women he dated, hating the thought of it. Was this her destiny? To live in his shadow, in the constant grip of jealous passion? She hated the thought of it and she hated herself for being caught in that trap like a fish in a net—seeing the freedom of open water, but powerless to reach it. She knew that it was this that made her terse with him, despite the fact that she wanted to at least appear nonchalant and relaxed.

She handed him his cup and he absent-mindedly grunted, not looking up at her.

'What the hell has been going on with this contract for Tony Harding?' he shot out, as she was preparing to leave the room and head for the quiet sanctuary of her own office. He looked at her, his eyes flicking over her quickly, then returning back to her face. Natalie suf-

fered the casual appraisal as equably as she could. Kane
Marshall appraised all women. It was part of his nature.
It did not signify any personal appreciation. Still, there
was something fleeting but worrying in those eyes as they
ran over body, something that she couldn't quite put her
finger on. She lowered her eyes, confused, not prepared
to dwell on it.

'He's halted it until some contractual queries are sorted
out,' Natalie replied smoothly, knowing immediately
what he was talking about. 'He's been asking for copies
of some minor variations to be made, but we have been
a bit long in getting back to him.'

'Why?'

Natalie shrugged. 'You'll have to speak to Roseanne
and Mr Douglas; they've been handling it in your
absence.'

'Or not, as the case may be.' He sat back and looked
at her rather longer this time, his eyes narrowed and calculating. 'Why didn't you take over?'

'I would have needed your say-so,' Natalie said
promptly.

He loosened his tie a notch further and she found her
eyes helplessly drifting towards the dark hairs just discernible on his chest. She impatiently pulled herself
together and produced a businesslike expression on her
face.

'How would you like to handle some of the smaller
accounts? From beginning to end? See them all the way
through? The more sensitive ones, like Tony Harding.'
He threw her a wry smile. 'I haven't got time for them
all.'

'Haven't you?' Natalie remarked innocently. 'You do
surprise me.'

'Sarcasm, Natalie?' He raised one eyebrow. 'Some bosses wouldn't stand for that, you know.'

Something in his voice suddenly confused her. Was he flirting? No. Her imagination. She relaxed and returned his teasing smile with a mocking one of her own.

'How lucky I am to have you for a boss, then,' she gushed, enjoying their rapport. 'Perhaps I ought to be paying you for the privilege instead of the other way around.'

'Seriously, Natalie. What do you think? Do you like the sound of my idea? It would be a promotion, and of course there would be a pay rise. I might even see my way to throwing in a company car as well.'

The offer had caught her by surprise. She looked at him levelly and saw that he was waiting for her response.

'Can I let you have my answer tomorrow?' she asked. Instead of the ready assent which she had expected, he frowned heavily and began fiddling with the fountain pen on his desk, tapping it on one of the files; then he gave an impatient sigh.

'Is that really necessary?' he snapped. 'I wouldn't have thought that you would have needed time to consider my proposition. In fact, most people would have jumped at it.'

Natalie stared at him, surprised. Was she being dense here? Was she missing something? She had thought her request the most natural thing in the world, but from his reaction anyone would have thought that she had asked for the impossible. What was going on here?

He stood up and prowled across to the large window behind his desk and stared down at the street below, his back to her, then he swung back around to face her, half perched on the window-sill, his arms folded across his chest.

'I'm only asking for one night to think it over,' Natalie informed him, still bemused.

'Why? Do you need to consult someone? Can't you make your mind up on your own?'

'I beg your pardon?'

'You heard me. I'm offering you the chance of a lifetime, with a pay rise to match——' he threw her a figure that made her inwardly gasp, then continued in the same flat, hard voice '—and you're not sure whether you want to accept it or not? Don't you think Eric will approve?'

Natalie's eyes widened. What was he on about now? Then the realisation dawned. Of course. He had seen them together, albeit in the company of someone else, someone who didn't count since she was Eric's sister and had been introduced to him as such, and had jumped to the wrong conclusion. He still thought that she had done something with herself because of a man. He couldn't understand the concept of a woman making the most of herself for herself.

Workwise he depended on her. This was his attempt to redefine his authority over her. Give her a promotion, make sure that she's not going anywhere, and life can carry on as normal.

Natalie stared at him with frozen politeness. It was on the tip of her tongue to inform him that Eric had nothing whatsoever to do with her request, then she thought, Why should I?

'Why should he disapprove?' she asked blandly.

He didn't care for that response. He preferred her to be uninvolved with a man. That was how she had been for the past five years and he had grown accustomed to it. She had always been able to fall in with his hours, his breakfast meetings, his weekend work at short notice.

He frowned but didn't reply and she said on a sigh,
'Look, if it means that much to you to have my answer
now, then I accept.'

He relaxed visibly. 'Personnel will fix up the new
contract.'

'I'll pop along there this afternoon,' Natalie promised.
Sometimes there was something boyishly transparent
about him. He moved back to his desk, but instead of
resuming work he continued to stare at her until Natalie
flushed awkwardly.

'Shall I get along to my desk?' she volunteered. 'I
might as well start sorting out my workload.'

He ignored her remark completely. 'So I was right after
all. Eric is the man in your life.'

Natalie shot him an impatient look and wondered
whether she could get away with telling him that she had
better things to do than stay in his office and discuss
some non-existent boyfriend. Then she decided that her
promotion really was too good to toss out of the window
in a fit of bravado. He might have given her the job for
all the wrong reasons, but that didn't mean that it wasn't
a damn good job and she had no intention of jeopard-
ising it.

'If you say so,' she said, glancing at her watch.

'What do you mean ''If I say so''? Is he or isn't he?'

'I wouldn't have thought that that was any of your
business,' she said, restraining the urge to snap. Her feet
were beginning to ache from standing up. She wanted
to get back to her desk, but she knew well enough that
that was impossible. Nothing incurred Kane's wrath more
easily than leaving before he was ready for you to leave.

'He looks as dull as dishwater,' he said with an ob-
lique glance in her direction, and Natalie bristled.

'Does he now?' she queried softly, angry on Eric's behalf even though she was not involved with him at all. What gave Kane Marshall the right to make snap judgements on anyone's personality anyway? It was hardly as though he was as unblemished as the driven snow.

'No need to get into a flap about it,' Kane said with infuriating calm. 'It was merely an observation.'

'I am not in a flap,' Natalie said stiffly, feeling very much like someone in a flap and wondering why. 'And since it's a free country you can make any number of observations that you like.'

He grinned at her and she glared back at him. 'I wouldn't have thought that he was your type at all, though,' he murmured, pursuing his line of thought with utter disregard for her tightened lips and glacial expression. 'Mind you, he does have a certain secure look, and women seem to yearn after security, for some peculiar reason.'

He lowered his eyes, the long, dark lashes drooping against his cheek and Natalie stared at him in frustration. He was deliberately provoking her and, like it or not, here she was, responding. Couldn't she do better than this, for heaven's sake?

'I don't yearn for security,' Natalie informed him. 'So much for your generalisations.'

'Don't you?' There was a mixture of curiosity and interest in his eyes when he looked up at her. 'You must be the exception to the rule in that case.'

'Or else you're completely off course in your sweeping comments about the female sex.' She smiled sweetly, feeling her composure return with reassuring speed, 'But no. I don't suppose you could be wrong. That would be unthinkable.'

He laughed at that, his eyes warm with appreciation for her verbal barb, and she had to force herself not to respond to him. And he talked about women wanting security? she thought. She certainly hadn't been lying when she told him that that was the furthest thing from her mind. Oh, no. Nothing as simple as a desire for security for her. Why settle for the easy course when she could waste her life secretly craving this sexy, arrogant, brilliant man sitting in front of her?

He glanced down at the file open in front of him, his hand on the telephone, and she knew that already his mind was back on work, after its short interlude wreaking havoc with her thoughts.

'Do you need any help with the transferral of accounts to you?' he asked, confirming her thoughts.

Natalie frowned. 'If you give me a list of the ones you want me to take over, I'll have a look at them this afternoon. I should be all right, but you might need to fill me in on any peculiarities with any of them.'

He nodded briefly. 'Tonight,' he said bluntly, already dialling his number. 'I take it you're no longer averse to overtime?'

'I never was,' Natalie said ambiguously.

'Fine.' He gave her a curt nod, his hand over the receiver. 'My place. Seven sharp. I'll get O'Leary to do something to eat.'

Natalie's mouth dropped open in dismay. This was not her idea of agreeable overtime one little bit. True, she had been to his flat before to work, usually in the presence of other people when she was used mainly to take the minutes and attend to practicalities. But it had always made her feel uneasy.

Poring over files with no one else around, apart from O'Leary, his manservant-cum-general housekeeper, who

was as deaf as post and generally retired to his quarters
to watch television as soon as he feasibly could anyway,
was not her idea of a fun night out.

'But...' Natalie began in protestation, but he was
already talking down the line, waving her away.

It wasn't until she was almost ready to leave for home
that she next got the opportunity to try and wheedle out
of the nightmarish scenario, but Kane was having none
of it.

'Three of the files are at my place. The most complicated three, in fact.' His eyes narrowed suspiciously
on her. 'Not trying to tell me that you can't work a bit
of overtime, are you? Because I needn't tell you that this
promotion will entail a fair amount of it. I won't allow
clock-watching.'

'Of course I understand,' Natalie said hastily, following him with her eyes as he prepared to leave for yet
another meeting, this time with one of his financial
directors.

'Good,' he said smoothly. 'In that case, there's no
problem, is there?'

'No problem,' she agreed with vast understatement.

She got home with barely enough time to have a bath
before she rushed back out. The phone was ringing as
she stepped out of the bath, and for one fleeting moment
of heady optimism she thought that it might be Kane
cancelling his engagement.

No such luck. It took her a second or two before she
recognised Eric's voice, then she remembered that she
had given him her telephone number, had agreed that
they mustn't lose touch. She rubbed herself dry, wan-
dering around the bedroom with the receiver tucked
behind one ear, awkwardly getting dressed in a pair of
jeans and a thin cotton top with buttons down the front.

In her left ear, Eric chatted to her enthusiastically until she gently interrupted to tell him that she was going out and would have to say goodbye. She knew that he was going to arrange to see her; after all, hadn't she given him every encouragement despite her 'hands off' warning? Even so, when he asked her to dinner later on in the week, she felt herself hesitate slightly.

Was it wise? Could she trust him? What if he wanted involvement, even though he had emphatically stated that it was the last thing on his mind?

Then she thought of Kane, the chiselled beauty of his features, the trail of women who flocked behind him, and on the spur of the moment she agreed with Eric that yes, dinner and the theatre would be wonderful.

'I'm afraid it'll have to be an early start,' he said. 'Can I meet you at your workplace? Say around six?'

It'll do me good, she thought, catching a taxi to Kane's flat in St John's Wood. She wasn't about to fall into the same old rut of all work and no play, promotion or no promotion. And Kane already knew of Eric's presence in her life. She would not have to explain anything further to him.

It was raining steadily outside and she let her thoughts drift as the taxi wound its way along Finchley Road, taking ages because the traffic was appalling. Wouldn't it be nice to live in the country? she thought. No traffic, no pollution, just wide open spaces. She had grown up in the country and although it was years since she had last lived there she still hankered for the peace and quiet.

Whenever she visited her sister in her delightful little house in Tamworth-in-Arden in the Midlands, she felt the same yen to pack in everything, Kane Marshall included, and do something really useful like become self-sufficient somewhere terribly rural.

Of course she wouldn't.

'You'd collapse from sheer boredom after a week,' her sister always told her, whenever her thoughts became a little too fanciful. 'London's in your blood now. You'll probably end up having to wean yourself out of it. Richmond first, then maybe Windsor, then the vegetable plot in the wilderness.'

But then vegetable plots in the middle of nowhere didn't include Kane, did they? Dammit, she thought, don't think like that! You're in the process of trying to exorcise him, or have you forgotten? Thinking along those lines isn't going to speed it up, is it?

She had to cover her head with her handbag when the taxi set her down outside Kane's flat. The steady drum of rain had become more of a downpour and she arrived on his doorstep soaking wet. O'Leary opened the door for her and she shouted by way of apology for removing her shoes in the hall.

'It's pouring outside! Don't want to bring my mud into the lounge!'

O'Leary took her jacket and said, shaking his head, 'Raining outside, is it?'

Obviously not wearing his hearing aid tonight, Natalie thought, her lips twitching. Most people would be mystified as to why Kane kept him on, but it didn't puzzle Natalie at all. Kane could be surprisingly indulgent in some areas and this was one of them. O'Leary had been with his family for years and when his parents retired to the South of France he had inherited the old man without question.

'Master Kane's in the lounge,' O'Leary was telling her, preceding her through the hall. 'Work, work, work— don't you young people ever know when to stop?'

Natalie knew better than to answer. Answering O'Leary without his hearing aid was an exercise in torture, so she clucked a bit and glanced around her. It really was a magnificent flat. It never ceased to impress her. The carpets were deep and in a soft, minty green colour, the walls, split by a dado rail in the middle, gave back the hues of green, but were mixed with creams and peaches as well, and were scattered with paintings, most of them impressionistic and all of them originals. Strange to think that someone as bold and self-assertive—in fact downright persuasive—as Kane Marshall could actually live in surroundings as restful as these.

O'Leary showed her into the lounge, yelling at Kane that the meal would be ready in half an hour sharp and could he please be prompt because there was a detective show on television that he wanted to watch.

'Oh, for God's sake,' Kane muttered, when O'Leary had departed, 'why on earth do I keep on that old duffer?' He turned towards the drinks cabinet and poured himself a gin and tonic for himself and a vodka and orange for her.

'Because it would break your heart to see him go.' Natalie accepted her drink, even though she would have preferred something non-alcoholic, and sipped from it tentatively.

'I must be mad,' he grumbled under his breath. 'I should have sent him packing off to the South of France with my parents.'

The files had been dumped on the marble coffee-table in front of the fireplace, and Natalie sauntered across to them, picking one up and rifling through it.

The sooner they got down to business, the sooner she would be on her way home. She was about to tactfully lever the conversation around to one of the accounts when she heard a silky voice from the doorway and looked up to see Anna standing there, barefoot, her blonde hair loose and trailing down her back in a mass of tendrils. The other woman was staring at her with open malice. 'Now I see why you cancelled our dinner date this evening,' she said with a freezing smile, stepping into the lounge and moving gracefully over to the sofa. She slipped into a pair of flat gold ballet shoes and turned towards Kane. 'Or maybe I don't.' A flick of a glance in Natalie's direction. 'If you've decided to supplant me with her, then your taste has certainly gone downhill.'

'This is work, Anna. Not that I have to justify cancelling a dinner date to you. So get your claws back in and wait for the taxi in silence like a good little girl.' Kane looked at Anna with a mixture of boredom and amusement.

'It's so *passé* to sleep with your secretary!' There was a hint of tears in her voice and Natalie checked the vigour of her retort back.

Kane glanced across at her, amused, and Natalie glared back with impotent fury. 'I am not sleeping with Mr Marshall,' she said tightly. 'I'm here to work, and in fact if it would ease things over I don't mind going right back home. Not one little bit.'

She bent to retrieve her handbag and Kane snapped, 'Stay put. Anna is the one who will be leaving.'

'I was looking forward to some time together,' Anna said in a smaller voice, and Natalie almost felt sorry for the other woman.

Kane shrugged. 'Work first, all else later.'

Anna bit her lower lip and threw Natalie a venomous look, then she said to Kane with a trembling smile, 'Darling, I forgot my bag upstairs. In your bedroom. Would you mind fetching it for me, please?'

He clicked his tongue impatiently, but left the room, and as soon as he was out Anna turned to Natalie. The trembling lip had gone, as had the broken, tearful voice.

'I might have guessed,' she said. 'You. Little Miss Background goes to grooming school and then thinks that she can steal my man. Well, you're in for a shock if that's what you're up to.'

CHAPTER THREE

NATALIE stared at the other woman, appalled.

'Up to?' she repeated faintly.

Anna walked towards her and Natalie took a step backwards, shamefacedly admitting to herself that an out-and-out fight was hardly on the cards, but not liking the expression on the other woman's face at all.

'Don't pretend that you don't know what I mean,' Anna spat, glancing backwards at the door to make sure that Kane had not put in a stealthy and unexpected appearance. This, Natalie knew instinctively, was precisely the sort of scene that would infuriate him. Two women, fighting like fisherwomen in the middle of his cool, elegant lounge. Or rather one woman fighting, the other gaping like a bemused goldfish.

'You're way off target.' Natalie gathered her wits together and made an effort to take control of the situation. 'I have no intention of taking your man, as you put it. Frankly, you're quite welcome to your man.' She grinned to herself. Kane would hate being referred to as Anna's man. As anyone's man, for that matter. Expressions like that had a proprietorial ring that he would not have approved of one little bit.

Ownership wasn't his style at all. He preferred to be totally free to come and go as he pleased, with whomever he pleased.

'I don't believe you.'

Natalie shrugged nonchalantly.

'Funny sort of coincidence,' Anna continued maliciously, 'this new you, who suddenly happens to find herself in Kane's apartment, for "work", isn't it? Ha. Do you think I was born yesterday?'

'Look,' Natalie said patiently, 'I *am* here to work.' She made a sweeping gesture towards the stack of files on the coffee-table. 'What do you think *they* are?' A new line in ornaments? she wanted to ask.

'Good grief. A bunch of stupid files. Well, you would need some kind of excuse for coming on to Kane, I suppose. And a few files are as good as any.'

Natalie's patience was beginning to evaporate. 'I am not interested in Kane Marshall,' she said angrily, 'and this conversation is ridiculous.'

'Not interested in Kane? Ha!' Anna's eyes narrowed on her. 'You've always been interested in him. Even when you were a podgy little thing hiding behind those great big spectacles of yours. So who are you trying to kid?'

There was a sharp silence, then Natalie turned away, concealing her trembling hands by picking up one of the files and studying it closely, then returning it to the coffee-table.

Had Anna meant that or had it been just a stab in the dark? If it had been just a stab in the dark, then it's accuracy was amazing. If, on the other hand, she had spoken from observation, then the consequences were not worth thinking about, because, Natalie thought, if Anna, flitting in and out of the office occasionally, had noticed her foolish love, then was Kane aware of it as well?

She wanted the ground to open up and swallow her up, or a sudden freak cyclone to whip her away to another planet. She said coolly enough, 'You have no idea what you're talking about. Your imagination's running riot because you're jealous, for no reason whatsoever, and I don't have to stay here and listen to you.' Where precisely she could retreat to was anyone's guess. She certainly had no intention of giving Anna the satisfaction of watching her run away, wounded. That would have been tantamount to admitting that there was something in what the other woman had said, for a start.

They heard the doorbell ring, then Kane's voice addressing the taxi driver, and Anna turned to face her quickly.

'I'm just warning you,' she bit out, 'keep your hands off him. I can't stop you watching, but he's mine.'

'Does he see it that way as well?'

Anna's face went bright red, then white. For a second, Natalie thought that that fight which she had nervously dismissed earlier on as being a ludicrous over-reaction to the situation might materialise after all, but it didn't.

'You think you're so clever,' she muttered, 'but if you make the mistake of trying to get your hands on Kane, then we'll see just who the clever one is.'

Kane appeared at the door, his eyes flicking expressionlessly between the two women, but already Anna was smiling at him and Natalie herself had something plastered across her face which she sincerely hoped resembled a relaxed grin as well.

'So nice to have had that little chat with you.' Anna oozed from her stronghold next to Kane.

'Wasn't it?' Natalie agreed, with as much control as she could muster, then she watched as Anna pulled Kane's head towards her and kissed him, long and hard and without any inhibitions whatsoever.

Natalie felt the sting of tears behind her eyes, foolish, foolish tears, but not a flicker of emotion crossed her face. What does she hope to achieve by that? she asked herself angrily. Does she think that I'm going to collapse in a jealous, writhing heap on the floor? Or maybe, and much more likely, she's just trying to let me know who owns who.

O'Leary appeared from behind them and shouted in exasperation, 'Taxi's here! Time to break all this up!'

Natalie just glimpsed Anna's look of irritation as she turned away and couldn't prevent a smile from crossing her face. Good old O'Leary, never one to be subtle. He practically hustled her out of the house, grumbling under his breath, turning around to yell to Kane that supper would be served in five minutes.

Kane shook his head ruefully at Natalie and strolled into the room, his hands thrust into his trouser pockets, his hair still slightly rumpled from where Anna's fingers had been coiled in it. Natalie viewed him with distaste.

'If I had known that I was intruding on something private, I would not have come here,' she said coolly, walking towards the dining-room with him, but making sure that there was a good distance between them.

'Intruding on something private? You make it sound as though you had caught me in bed with her.' He laughed under his breath, obviously delighted at the expression of stiffness on her face, and Natalie wanted to scream in frustration.

'I got the distinct impression that I would have if I had turned up a few minutes later,' she muttered. 'Or does she normally wander around the flat with her shoes off?' God, she thought with an inward groan, I sound like a jealous wife. The last thing in the world I want to do is to let him think that I actually give a damn what he does in his private life, yet here I am, only a hair's breadth away from sounding shrewish and possessive.

She glanced around the dining-room, and made a
bright remark about the décor, asking him whether he
had had it changed recently, even though she knew that
he hadn't.

'As a matter of fact,' he commented casually, ignoring her attempt to change the conversation, 'she does
tend to take her shoes off when she's here. I suppose it
has something to do with the ridiculous height of those
things that she sticks on her feet. At least I don't have
to suffer the irritation of watching *you* hobble around
the office in five-inch heels because you think, for some
obscure reason, they look glamorous. You may have
changed some things, but I'm pleased to see that others
have remained the same.'

They sat at the table, opposite each other, and O'Leary
brought them in their starters of avocado with vinaigrette dressing. Home-made vinaigrette dressing. He was,
surprisingly, an excellent cook. She dug into her avocado
and made light, non-threatening conversation with him,
discussing what was playing at the theatres in London,
what new films were out, food.

'I really was surprised to see you in that restaurant
the other evening,' he commented suddenly. He had finished his starter and she could feel his green eyes fixed
on her downbent head, surveying her. 'Do you go there
often?'

'First time,' Natalie answered briefly. 'It's only just
recently opened,' she added, when he made no comment.

'So it has,' he agreed. 'It was recommended to me by
the Maison Française. It's their sister restaurant.'

'Is it?' she said politely.

'What surprised me even more, though, was that you
would invite a third party on your dinner date out.'

She looked up to meet his eyes, which were amused and curious. He had always got a kick out of quizzing her on her personal life, knowing that it irritated her when he did it. She had a feeling that trying to imagine her with her hair down, dancing till dawn, had appealed to his sense of humour. Probably because it would have been so vastly different from how she appeared to him when she was at work.

Now something had shifted slightly. The image would not have been so very different from what he saw during working hours, and having caught her in a restaurant had clearly whetted his appetite to find out more about her private life. He was playing games with her and she didn't see why she should respond. She ignored him and meticulously concentrated on finishing her starter.

'Delicious,' she said.

'Delicious,' he agreed, with a mocking edge in his voice.

'You're very lucky, having O'Leary to cook for you. Most single men either end up eating out all of the time or else living off take-away food.'

'By most single men, I take it to mean that you're talking about the riveting Eric?'

There was something insolent lurking under the politeness and it sparked an angry reaction in her. He was so conceited! Eric might not set the world on fire, but he was safe. There was a lot to be said for safety.

O'Leary came in to clear away their dishes, and then busied himself with the main course, a simple affair of lamb steaks with mustard sauce and new potatoes. And, Natalie was relieved to note, his temporary invasion into her private life was dropped. He began discussing work, and she immediately relaxed. This was familiar territory and she asked a string of questions about her new role, quizzing him on the accounts she would be handling. She already knew a great deal about them anyway, and Kane methodically filled her in on things which were not necessarily in the file. He knew all the directors of the companies personally, and he made her giggle with his stories about them.

This, she thought suddenly, was the essence of his charm, this extraordinary ability to make a woman feel as though she was at the centre of his universe, even when she meant nothing more to him than an insignificant working companion.

Poor Anna. No wonder she was so desperate to hang on to him. Couldn't she see for herself that, however witty and sexy and clever he might be, he was not about to be tamed? Presumably he would get married one day, but only when it suited him, and probably to someone who could bring with her more significant assets than a good body and an undemanding intellect.

Still, when did love ever listen to logic? She, Natalie, of all people should know that no amount of careful reasoning could control that wild patter of her heart whenever he was around. Anna did not give the impression that serious thought and an ability to reason were strong points with her, but who could tell?

They had a dessert of *crème brûlée*, and Natalie said without thinking, 'I could go to bed right now.'

Her eyes met his, recognised the unspoken speculative question in them, and looked away in confusion.

'Shall we have coffee in the lounge?' he asked, amused to have addled her. 'Might as well cover the rest of the ground on these accounts, then you can take your sweet self off to bed.' He shot her a half-wicked, half-innocent look which Natalie pretended not to notice.

They had shared a bottle of wine over dinner, and what with the vodka and orange beforehand Natalie felt her eyelids drooping as she surveyed the files in the lounge. She was quite unused to alcohol. One glass of wine made her feel heady. Right now she could fall asleep without any problem whatsoever. She summoned up her energy and listened in frowning concentration while he pointed out the important facts in the files, but she couldn't help a feeling of relief when he shut the last one and informed her that school was over.

Instead of rushing to her feet, Natalie relaxed back in the chair, a smile of contentment playing on her lips, and sipped from the cup of coffee.

'You never answered my question,' Kane said, his green eyes flicking over her body and then resting on the soft, gentle lines of her face.

'Question?' Natalie laughed slightly and half closed her eyes. 'What question?' Her head felt pleasantly fuzzy. It was almost too much trouble to think and it was certainly too much trouble to be on her guard.

'Why did you and your boyfriend have company on your romantic evening out? Whatever happened to young lovers whispering sweet nothings in each other's ears?' He took a mouthful of coffee and looked at her over the rim of the cup.

The distant clang of alarm bells rang in her head. The question was harmless enough, if a bit impertinent. It was the atmosphere which had become dangerous. Natalie recognised that somewhere in the muddled recesses of her brain, but somehow couldn't seem to get up the energy to do anything about it.

'Is that what you do with Anna?' she heard herself asking and he shot her a lazy, charming smile.

'I outgrew sweet nothings quite some time ago.'

'What a shame,' Natalie remarked.

'Why?'

I shouldn't be encouraging this, Natalie thought. He can handle it, but I can't. She blinked and sat up a bit straighter, but the suddenness of the movement didn't seem to have the desired effect. She raised one eyebrow in irony. 'If you don't know, then I can't help but feel a little sorry for you. After all, there's a lot more to a relationship than sex.'

The amusement left his face for an instant and he gave her a blank look. 'Really?' He appeared to give the matter some thought, then he said slowly, 'Though now that you mention it I do recall a time when I would have agreed with you.'

'When was that?' she asked, with genuine curiosity.

'When I was about fifteen. Her name was Laura and I thought that she had descended directly from the heavens. I think the word for it was infatuation.'

'And what happened?'

'To Laura? She changed schools and vanished out of my life forever. Probably married now with a litter of children. And as for infatuation—it gave way to experience.' His voice was bitter, though still light. He poured himself another cup of black coffee and proceeded to survey it contemplatively, his finger tracing the rim. 'I found out that the more money one has, the more women's attitudes undergo a change.'

'I think that's called human nature. Shame that you allowed it to jade you.' Natalie couldn't believe what she was saying. The words were coming out of her mouth and it was as if she, personally, had had no hand in forming them.

'You make me feel about a hundred,' he said, and the bitterness had left his voice. That teasing, amused tone was back, re-establishing the balance between them. 'You always have. And what about you? One confidence deserves another, don't you think? I know so much about you, maybe more than I've ever known about any woman in my life, but there are all sorts of gaps. For instance, were you ever the victim of infatuation?'

Natalie could feel the blood rush to her head. What would he say if she confessed to him where her own personal agonies lay? Would he laugh? Feel sorry for her? He said that he knew her, and he did, just as she knew him, with all his quirks and habits that had managed over the years to embed themselves in her, but that very special knowledge that sprang from true intimacy wasn't there.

'Of course I was,' she murmured, looking away. 'But it can be lonely when you're not in the beauty-queen stakes.' She challenged him with her eyes.

'Beauty is a personal thing.'

'Is that why your women are all physically perfect?' she couldn't resist saying, and he shot her a quizzical look from under his lashes.

'Beauty and physical perfection are quite different, though,' he said softly. 'You have your own special beauty; you always have.'

Natalie blushed and stood up, a little shakily. 'I really must be going now.' She wanted to inform him, quietly and calmly, that she wasn't so stupid to be taken in by words like that, but she could barely muster a coherent sentence together.

'Already?' His eyebrows shot up in surprise. 'What about a nightcap? I was enjoying chatting to you. You relax me, believe it or not.'

'No. No nightcap, thank you,' she said too quickly. 'Perhaps you could get O'Leary to call me a cab?'

He did, and while they waited he poured himself a glass of brandy, swallowing it back in one gulp. 'Sure you won't join me?' he repeated his offer and she shook her head with a smile.

'I want to make sure that I have a clear head for tomorrow.'

'You're putting on your secretarial clothes again,' Kane remarked drily, moving over to where she was standing, looming over her until she felt as if she was going to suffocate under the weight of his masculinity. Natalie laughed awkwardly and their eyes met. Her breath caught in her throat. He was so tall, so overpowering, so devastatingly good-looking.

Before she could look away, his head swooped down to hers and his mouth brushed over hers, finding it warm and soft and pliant. It was the first time he had ever kissed her. True, at Christmas-time, he would give her an impersonal, light-hearted embrace, as he did with other female members of his staff. But nothing like this. Even though he barely touched her mouth with his own there was nothing at all impersonal about his action. In fact, there was something strangely, deeply intimate about it.

He drew back, looking down at her, and Natalie realised with a mixture of disgust and dismay that she was trembling. Like a gauche teenager being kissed for the first time. Which wasn't that far off the truth. Her experience with men was limited, and for the past five years, ever since Kane had stepped into her life and taken over her emotions, not at all.

She knew now with a sense of shock how deeply she had been holding herself for just this one kiss. A kiss that meant nothing to him at all.

She couldn't say a word. He bent over her again and this time his mouth met hers in a kiss that was more demanding, fiercer. He was gripping her by her shoulders, pulling her against him so that she could feel his hard arousal pressed against her. With a sigh of pleasure she felt his hand move to curl into her hair. There were no words she could find to describe the sensations coursing through her body. It was as if she had been starved for years, for a lifetime, and now she had been given a taste of food.

Of course it was madness. The ring of the doorbell announcing her taxi brought her back to her senses and reality hit her like a bucket of cold water. She pulled herself out of his arms and took a few deep breaths, trying to stabilise herself. She could feel tears of anger and humiliation pricking the back of her eyes and she had to blink very quickly to make sure that they did not fall. She had made enough of a fool of herself for one night already, without that.

'My taxi's here,' she said huskily, not looking at him.

'You could always send him away,' Kane murmured softly, and this time she did look at him, stunned.

'Are you mad?'

She turned away and began hunting around the room for her handbag.

'Are you looking for this?' Kane asked from behind her, and she turned around to see him dangling the bag from his finger, a lazy smile on his lips.

Very funny, she thought. What a jolly laugh you must be having at my expense. She snatched the bag from him and he laughed softly, his eyes alight with dry amusement.

'I'm glad you find this whole situation so entertaining,' she said through gritted teeth.

'I'm sorry,' he apologised, without a hint of sorrow in his voice. The smile died from his lips and he said more seriously, 'Actually, entertaining isn't quite the word I would use.'

No, I'm sure it isn't, she wanted to retort. Perhaps interesting would be a better word, an interesting little experiment in shocking the respectable little secretary.

'I'd better go,' she said quietly. 'It's quite late now. Shall I carry the files home with me or will you take them in tomorrow morning?'

'I'll bring them in with me,' he said, following her to the door.

O'Leary was at the front door, and he glared at the both of them, as if blaming them for having to get out of bed.

'Goodbye,' Natalie said politely, in control now. She made to move away, but before she could Kane's fingers curled around her elbow, and he said softly, his green eyes betraying no expression whatsoever,

'I know you want to pretend that what happened just then didn't, but I think you ought to consider your relationship with this Eric chap very carefully if I am capable of arousing you the way that I did.' He paused and Natalie controlled the urge to commit first-degree murder. 'Are you serious about him?' he asked with a sudden flush.

With an effort, her grey eyes met his steadily. 'Yes,' she said with a sudden spurt of inspiration. 'Yes, as a matter of fact I am. And, just to set the record straight, I may have felt something just then, in the heat of the moment, but I very much doubt it had a great deal to do with you.' She stopped and thought briefly about what she was going to say next. 'I'm afraid I can't take alcohol. It makes me muddle-headed; I tend to act out of character after a couple of glasses of wine.' She gave a tinkling laugh as if to imply, Dear me, I hate to shatter your ego, but... and continued, 'You could have been anyone.'

That, she thought, had to be one of the biggest lies she had ever told, but the situation demanded it. She had every intention of walking out of this apartment with her dignity intact, at least in the eyes of Kane Marshall, and if that meant telling a few white lies, then so be it.

'Could I?' he said grimly. 'Shall we put that to the test, my darling, dedicated little secretary?'

Natalie felt a rush of hot colour flood her cheeks, but she stood her ground, and when she replied there was not so much as a quiver in her voice, even though her heart was thudding painfully in her chest.

'I don't think that that's in my job description, do you?'

There was no answer to that one. He stared down at her, and then moved on towards the front door, where he told the taxi driver, in curt tones, to charge the fare to the Marshall company account. The taxi driver grinned. He had done business with Kane Marshall before. He worked for the firm who dealt with all the Marshall Corporation travel. Now he surreptitiously scanned Natalie's face with interest, and she looked away, quite aware of what was going through his head.

How many other women had he picked up from this address? He assumed that she was one in the usual line.

'I'll see you in the morning, Mr Marshall,' Natalie said, pointedly emphasising the Mr so that no one was in any doubt that her relationship with Kane Marshall was not a sexual one.

He gave her a mocking smile and drawled, 'Of course, Miss Robins,' then he vanished into the interior of the house and she slipped into the taxi, glad for the opportunity to gather her thoughts together, even though she didn't care for them at all.

She was still shaking from what had happened inside there. It had been a disaster on an unthinkable scale, because there was so much more at stake then simply her pride. If it had just been her pride, she could have walked away and in due course slotted the whole incident to the back of her mind. A mistake. An unfortunate one, but nevertheless nothing that could not be relegated to that safe category of invaluable experience.

But she was in love with Kane Marshall. Something that was unimportant to him now threatened to consume her. One thing for sure—she was not going to let him get any ideas into his head. She had told him that her response was due to the heady carelessness brought on by the alcohol and she was going to stick to that excuse as if her life depended on it. At least she had had the foresight to imply that her heart was tied up elsewhere, namely with Eric.

She thought of solid, nice, amiable Eric and wondered whether his ears were burning right now. He would have an apoplectic fit over his calculator if he knew that he was now a major participant in an imaginary love-affair. The thought brought a watery smile to her lips.

By the time she got into work the following morning, she had made up her mind that she would handle the situation if it killed her.

It helped that Kane was nowhere around. He had left a scribbled note for her on her desk, informing her that he had been called to an urgent meeting at their Paris headquarters and would be back later on in the week.

Natalie stared at the black writing with a feeling of relief. Coping was much easier without him around.

She spent the rest of the day solidly working on her accounts, liaising with various managers, as well as fitting in the personnel officer, and was pleasantly exhausted by the time she returned to her flat.

Eric phoned to make sure that she had not forgotten about their date later in the week, and remained on the telephone chatting for quite a while. Despite what she had said to him, was he already becoming more involved with her than either of them wanted? she wondered, as she thoughtfully replaced the receiver a while later. It was flattering to be pursued by someone, and especially by someone with whom she found it so easy to relate. Maybe, she thought, she should not try quite so hard to cut herself off from the opportunity for involvement.

What, after all, was the point of never looking twice at another man? Of never giving anyone the chance to get close to her? Hadn't that been one of the decisions which she had made in Kane's absence? She resolved to let her relationship with Eric take its course.

The thought clung to her at the back of her mind for the remainder of the week, and on the Friday, when she was due to be collected by him at the office, she spent longer than usual in the morning trying various outfits. She wanted something that was attractive without being pushy. She would also have to wear it to the office, so really a skin-tight scarlet catsuit was totally out of the question. Not that she possessed anything along those lines anyway, nor would she want to.

In the end, she settled for a close-fitting cream silk skirt, which finished just above the knees, and a black and white checked sleeveless top, also in silk.

It was a relief, she thought, as six o'clock rolled around, that Eric was picking her up at the office when he was. Silk was definitely not suited to extensive daytime wear, however comfortable the outfit was. She was just too conscious of being over-dressed to relax comfortably.

She was absorbed transferring some information from one of the files on to her computer when the outer door opened and she looked up, a warm smile on her lips. Kane's eyes surveyed her sardonically but before she could say anything Eric appeared behind him and alongside him was Anna, her blonde hair tied up in a style that looked as though it had taken several days to accomplish.

'Natalie,' Eric said warmly, moving towards her and stretching out his hand. 'I bumped into your boss and his girlfriend in the elevator.' He went red. 'Hence the mass arrival. Sorry I'm a bit late.'

'Are you?' Natalie glanced at her watch in surprise and realised that she had been so engrossed in what she had been doing that the time had slipped by. It was a little after six-fifteen. She stood up, her cheeks pink as Eric's eyes gleamed with appreciation.

'You look charming,' he breathed, and from behind him Anna said in a brittle voice,

'What a sweet little outfit. It suits you. Darling——' she turned towards Kane '—doesn't she look sweet? I used to have an outfit similar to that when I was a bit younger but——' she giggled a little '—it always made me feel as though I should be behind a typewriter.'

Kane didn't respond to that biting observation. He looked from Eric to Natalie, his eyes finally settling on Natalie's face, and said casually, 'And where are you two lovebirds off to tonight?'

'Theatre and supper afterwards,' Natalie said, moving to link her arm through Eric's. 'And what about you two?' she added politely, fetching her black bag and tugging Eric gently towards the door.

Anna answered with a smug smile, 'Oh, nothing quite as adventurous as the theatre. I'm thinking of something altogether more intimate.' Laughter gurgled in her throat.

'Well, have a good time,' Natalie said, without flinching. She looked at Kane blandly. 'I'll see you on Monday. Have a nice weekend.'

And that, she thought as she strolled out of the office with Eric, was handled very nicely indeed. No stupid blushing. She had been cool, confident and highly secretarial. If only she could control herself with such aplomb all of the time.

She glanced across at Eric, suddenly grateful for his undemanding maleness. He met her eyes and smiled.

'Do you know something, Natalie?' he asked, and she shook her head, puzzled. 'I think you and I are going to become very friendly indeed. I think that fate was definitely at work when I accepted my sister's invitation to dinner with the two of you the other evening.'

Natalie laughed slightly. 'Fate?' she said drily. 'My experiences with fate don't have much of a track record, but who knows? Maybe the tide is turning.'

Remember, she told herself, give yourself a chance. It's the only way to purge Kane Marshall from your system.

CHAPTER FOUR

WASN'T it funny the way everyone had their own story to tell?

From the outside, Eric was the height of staidness. He gave the impression of a man who always thought before he acted, who never did anything rashly or in the heat of the moment. Even his choice of play had been slightly unadventurous. A popular West End musical rather than a lesser known production being staged at one of the fringe theatres.

But over the meal, a pleasant Italian restaurant which obviously catered for theatre-goers and adjusted their prices accordingly, Eric had confided in her, a little at first, then much more as the bottle of wine lowered both their inhibitions and made them more comfortable with each other.

Natalie had listened with interest. She had no desire to pry into his personal life, but he had clearly wanted to talk to her about it, and she was adept at being a sympathetic ear. She listened while he told her about his two-year infatuation with a model. He had only just begun his accountancy training course and his parents had been appalled by his choice of girlfriend, but he had adored her. There had been something larger than life about her, maybe because she was so physically exquisite.

'Isn't it weird,' he had told her over dinner, 'how easy it is to lose your heart to someone totally unsuitable?' and Natalie had nodded with heartfelt agreement. Wasn't she a victim of the same mistake? At least Eric had emerged from his.

It transpired, over coffee, that his dream woman had walked out on him without so much as a note after their two-year affair. His disillusionment somehow made Natalie warm towards him, maybe because it created an intangible bond between them, even though she told him nothing about her own foolish love for Kane.

At any rate, they had parted company shortly after midnight having arranged to see each other again the following weekend.

'Just friends,' Natalie had reminded him at her front door.

'Just friends,' he had agreed, and they had looked at each other with mutual, unspoken understanding. He had no love to give her, and that suited her just fine because she had none to give him. But on a platonic level they had ignited from the word go, and she had no misgivings about seeing him again.

She was still feeling pleasantly content as she let herself into her office the following Monday morning. Kane was already in, and rummaging around her desk. He looked up as she entered.

'Had a good weekend, I take it?' he drawled. 'You look as though you're about to burst forth into song any minute now.'

'Good morning,' Natalie replied. She approached her desk, doing her best not to be overawed by his presence there. 'What are you looking for? Perhaps I can help you?'

'The Mallory account.'

Natalie turned away and fished it expertly out of the filing cabinet and handed it to him with a wry expression on her face.

'I thought I left it on your desk on Friday evening.'

'You did. I cleared it away.'

'Very efficient. Now I know why I pay you as much as I do.' He remained standing by her desk, the file in one hand, his other hand stuck into his trouser pocket, until Natalie asked hesitantly,

'Is there something else?'

'All ready to start working on those accounts today?' She nodded, wondering how she could manoeuvre herself to her desk without bumping into him. 'Good,' he said, not budging, 'good.'

Natalie finally raised one eyebrow questioningly. 'Do I get the feeling that there's something else on your mind?'

'What gives you that idea?'

'Normally you barely have time to stand still for longer than five minutes during the day. You must want to tell me something, or else you wouldn't be by my desk. You'd probably be in your office, shouting orders.'

'Well,' he smiled drily, 'there is something I'd like to mention to you. Nothing very important. Could you come into my office?' He spun round and Natalie followed in his wake, closing the office door behind her.

'Sit down,' he said, adding, 'please,' after a few moments. When she had first gone to work for him, he had been quite accustomed to issuing commands without even the slightest regard for courtesy. Natalie had informed him in no uncertain terms that she had no intention of being treated like a skivvy, and he had wryly acceded to her request for politeness.

That was five years ago. What, she wondered, must he have thought of that plump, plain girl telling him off in the confines of his own office?

He began fiddling with his fountain pen and chatting to her about details of some of the workload she was about to inherit, but Natalie had the oddest feeling that he was merely skirting around what he really wanted to say.

She couldn't imagine why but she was suspicious enough to think that if he couldn't get to the point without a ten-minute preamble, then whatever he wanted to tell her wasn't about to fill her with glee. It was unlike him to tread carefully. So why, she thought nervously, the sudden attack of sensitivity? Was she about to get the sack? She searched her brain for what she might have done but came up with a blank.

Finally, when there was a lull in the one-way conversation, she looked at him squarely in the face and said, 'You mentioned quite a bit of this when I saw you the other evening. Is there something else you want to say?'

'Do I conclude from that that I'm being repetitive?' He grinned at her and she reluctantly smiled back, relaxing.

'It's been known to affect people as they grow older,' she suggested seriously, and he burst out laughing.

'Thank you very much,' he said. 'I'm a way off collecting my pension yet, though.' His eyes gleamed. 'In fact, some would say that I'm in the prime of my life.'

'Would they?' It was an effort to meet his stare without blushing, but Natalie managed it, knowing that he would find any embarrassment on her part highly entertaining.

'Wouldn't you?' he asked curiously, and Natalie ignored the question. Responding to that one definitely was over and beyond the call of duty.

'Is there anything else?' she asked pointedly and he sat back in the swivel chair, surveying her from under long, dark lashes.

'Just one thing,' he murmured, and Natalie thought, At last, the reason why I was asked in here in the first place. 'It's of a personal nature,' he continued, his eyes not leaving her face, and she felt a wary tingle race down her spine.

'Is it?'

'There's no need to look so worried,' he informed her and Natalie frowned. 'It's about your boyfriend.'

'Eric?'

Kane nodded slowly. 'I'm not in the business of offering advice to other people on how to handle their love lives, but we've worked together for a long time, and I wouldn't like to see you get hurt.' He paused, then continued before she could open her mouth to speak, 'He's not your type.'

There was a long silence while Natalie stared at him incredulously. 'I beg your pardon?' she finally said. 'I don't think I heard correctly.'

'Now, now,' he murmured soothingly, with a little half-smile, 'there's no need to be offended.'

She gritted her teeth and wondered how long she would get in prison for manslaughter. 'Offended?' she offered with heavy sarcasm. 'Because the guru on love is offering me advice on my love life? Why on earth should I be offended?' She gave a high little laugh. 'I should be flattered.'

'I'm glad you see it that way,' Kane agreed lazily. 'As I said, I'm not in the habit of giving advice, but you're not terribly experienced, and I shouldn't like you to become involved with a man when really you're not suited to each other at all.'

'And you've managed to deduce all this from a casual meeting?' Natalie asked coldly. 'How clever.'

Kane shrugged. 'It's quite obvious. The man's as dull as dishwater. He's probably after a woman who will marry him, give up her career, have two point two children and settle comfortably into mediocrity.'

'And what makes you think that that's not precisely what I would like to do?'

'Because I know you.' He shot her a crooked smile.

'You don't know me at all,' Natalie informed him, wishing that there were some depths to which she could allude, some secret and highly exciting facet of her life which she could carelessly toss in his face to wipe that smug smile away. But there wasn't.

'Of course I know you,' he refuted, in that same, implacably calm voice. 'We've worked together for five years. I've seen all different sides of you. Do you remember how nervous you were when your sister got married? You were convinced that you'd make a fool of yourself as chief bridesmaid.'

'You try being chief bridesmaid at your sister's wedding!' Natalie defended hotly. 'You'd understand how I felt!' She wished now that she had been more circumspect in her dealings with the damn man. Trust him to drag up a detail like that and use it against her.

He drew a circle on the notepad in front of him then patterned it with vague, concentric doodles, his eyes not on her face.

'What I'm trying to say here is that I know you better than you think. There was a time,' he said accusingly, 'when you would have confided in me, instead of treating me like the enemy.'

So that was it, Natalie thought suddenly. He was jealous of the fact that he could no longer feel in charge of my life. The thought hurt and thrilled her at the same time.

'I'm not treating you like an enemy,' she responded automatically.

'You act as though I'm prying into your affairs.'

'You *are* prying into my affairs!'

'There you go again.'

Natalie sighed wryly. And they said that women were illogical? Right now she was finding it difficult to keep up with this man's thread of reasoning.

He gave her a sly look. 'I'm sure you like him, but I can't imagine that you feel passionate about him.'

Natalie's mouth dropped open. 'Th-that's none of your business,' she stuttered angrily. 'Thank you so much for the advice, I'm sure you meant well, but I can handle my own love life, thank you very much. And for your information,' she threw at him, 'I happen to feel very passionate about Eric, as he does about me.' So there, she wanted to add.

An expression of surprise crossed his features, and Natalie rushed on triumphantly, 'We're extremely passionate about each other. Now, is that all?'

'It is,' Kane said tautly. There was insolent disbelief in his eyes and Natalie turned away, feeling drained. Her hand was on the doorknob when he said as an after-thought, 'What are you doing over the weekend?'

'Why?' she asked cautiously.

'Business, actually,' he said drily, looking up from his papers. 'I'll be entertaining a few clients on Saturday evening at my country house and I need you to be there. You can get there about six and make sure that every-thing's all right in the kitchen. No need for caterers. Josie's going to do the lot and O'Leary will be giving her a hand.' He winced. 'I have to say something about being on best behaviour. I can't have prospective clients being shown the door by O'Leary because he doesn't happen to care for the cut of their suit. You know how unpredictable he can be.'

He returned to his paperwork, effectively dismissing her, and Natalie remained where she was.

'I'm afraid I can't come,' she said finally and his head shot up.

'Can't come?'

'I've made other arrangements.'

'This seems to be becoming a habit,' he snapped, staring at her. 'I thought I made it quite clear when you were given that promotion that working overtime was not debatable.'

'I have no objections to working overtime,' Natalie said with a sigh, 'you know that. It's just that this is very last-minute and...' Her voice trailed off and his eyes dropped a shade cooler.

'Well, I do beg your pardon,' Kane said acidly. 'Next time I'll do my level best to arrange important meetings to fit in with your free time.'

'Can't you get a replacement for me?'

'You know I can't. You know most of these people personally. Two of them will be dealing with you directly from now on. You'll just have to cancel whatever you arranged. What did you have planned anyway?'

Natalie wondered whether she should tell him quite bluntly that that was definitely none of his business, then she erred on the side of caution. 'Eric and I had arranged to spend the weekend together,' she confessed.

'Hardly what I would call an irrevocable arrangement,' Kane pointed out and Natalie's eyes flashed rebelliously.

'I was looking forward to it,' she said tightly. 'I know that work comes first with you, but other people don't work along those lines.'

'It was never a problem before,' he pointed out coldly, 'and if it's a problem now, then you're in the wrong job.'

'Are you trying to tell me something?'

He stood up and raked his hands through his hair, looking as though he could shake her.

'Don't be a little fool. Look,' he said, 'why don't you bring him? That way I could have you where I need you and lover boy could be in the background as well.'

Natalie stared at him helplessly. Didn't the man ever give up?

'Don't tell me that you're embarrassed to bring him along,' Kane drawled, when she didn't immediately respond to his suggestion, and she glared at him.

'Of course not! It's just that...'

'A weekend entertaining clients isn't the height of romance?'

That thought had actually been the furthest thing away from her mind, but she decided that it was as good enough an excuse for her hesitation as any other, so she nodded.

Kane looked at her, amused. 'You can see it as a challenge. I have managed to find romance in far less prepossessing situations.'

Natalie didn't want to hear this at all. It set her mind whirring far too feverishly for its own good. She met the amused green eyes blankly, and realised with resignation that there was no point in fighting him. He had made his plans, to include her, and there was no way that he was going to allow her to get out of them.

And she could see the way he was thinking. She had always been able to fit in with whatever he had asked of her in the past. As far as he was concerned, the presence of Eric was a minor technicality, nothing that couldn't be resolved, certainly nothing that should intrude on the far more pressing business of work.

'Besides,' Kane said to her, 'Anna will be there. As will the other halves of the people I've invited. He won't be a fish out of water, if that was concerning you.'

'Not at all,' Natalie denied quickly. 'Eric could handle himself in any situation.' Good grief, she thought, this is getting beyond a joke.

'Very loyal.'

'How many people will be there?' she asked, changing the subject.

'Twelve in all,' he told her. 'Hence the fact that I'm not calling in the caterers.' He listed the people invited and she made a face when he got to one of the women, a married lady who made no pretence to hide the fact that she was attracted to Kane. He correctly read the expression on her face and grinned.

'That's why Anna's coming.'

'Sorry?' Natalie said, flushing at the ease with which he read her mind.

'Protection from Mrs Jarvis. I can see from your face that you've noticed her lack of tact, shall we call it, on the past occasions that we've met.'

He didn't look in the slightest bit flattered or surprised by the unwanted attentions of a married woman, but then he wouldn't, would he? Natalie thought ironically. He was quite accustomed to attention from all quarters.

'I thought it might have been in my imagination,' Natalie lied awkwardly. It was this empathy with him that undermined her most.

'Hardly. She invited me to sleep with her the last time we met. I don't think she was too impressed when I refused. I told her I had made a prior arrangement to wash my hair.'

Natalie looked at him, incredulous, until he laughed out loud.

'Horrified? I'm surprised. I thought you were highly versed in the realms of passion.' There was a thread of laughter in his voice and the stony look on her face amused him even further. There were times, she thought, when she positively hated him. Now was one of those times.

It was clear from the look on his face that he didn't believe a word about her passionate affair with Eric. In fact, the thought was so ludicrous that it made him laugh. Beneath the anger at his response there was a well of hurt which she refused to acknowledge. She waited in silence until his amusement subsided, then she left the office, still fuming.

The man was unbearable. How could she ever have fallen in love with someone who was so unbearable?

It was a rhetorical question, of course. She knew why she had fallen in love with him. He might be infuriatingly self-assured but he was also clever and witty and had a sense of humour which had edged its way under her skin until the thought of ever having to live without it made her go cold.

Still, that didn't mean that she was looking forward to a weekend at his country house entertaining clients, with the delightful Anna swanning around and making sly, derisory comments at her expense.

It was funny but when she had been overweight and not particularly appealing she had managed these dos without any bother at all. She had slotted herself comfortably into the background and had happily fulfilled her duties, observing Kane from a distance, knowing that she was virtually invisible to him. Now something had changed. Perhaps it was all in her mind, but an element of sexuality had entered their relationship which disturbed her, made her all the more aware of how dangerous her position was. She was playing with fire merely by continuing to work for him, and playing with fire inevitably involved burnt fingers. Hers.

She half expected Eric to decline Kane's invitation, but to her surprise he accepted with alacrity, informing her that it might prove a very good opportunity to make valuable contacts.

Natalie hadn't thought of that. She grinned wryly to herself as she replaced the receiver, and decided that it was just as well that she was not madly in love with him because she would have been quite disappointed at the speed with which he relinquished a weekend alone in her company in favour of the chance to make a few contacts.

The following morning Kane asked her whether she had sorted out the weekend with Eric and she nodded, not glancing in his direction.

'We'll be there at six,' she informed him, skimming through her mail and then getting up to make them both a cup of coffee.

'I half expected you to tell me that he had refused to spend a weekend watching you entertain my clients,' Kane called out, walking towards his office. 'Odd sort of response considering the passion you two share. Or rather the passion you claim you two share. Or maybe my definition of passion isn't quite the same as yours, because I know that if I were Eric I damn well wouldn't want to share you for a weekend.'

Natalie dumped the cup of coffee on his desk. 'Well, you're not Eric, are you?' she said sweetly, her skin burning from his throw-away remark which had sent a series of images shooting through her brain.

He grinned wickedly at her and promptly dropped the subject, but his reaction had left her with a niggling feeling. Whatever he said, however he behaved, deep down he would never equate her with anything other than the sexless secretary, she thought. She might drag Eric along, but he didn't for a minute think that he would distract her from her duties because despite what she had told him he had not believed a word about any of it.

She was preparing to leave for home on the Friday when the outer door opened and she looked up to see Anna staring down at her.

'Mr Marshall isn't here,' Natalie informed her without bothering with niceties, which she knew would have met with a brick wall anyway. 'He had a meeting in the Midlands and he won't be back this evening.'

'He didn't tell me,' Anna said, piqued.

'It was a sudden thing.' Natalie strapped her bag over her shoulder and switched off her computer terminal.

'Well, I'll see him tomorrow, anyway.' Anna shrugged but didn't move. 'Kane tells me that you will be there with that boyfriend of yours.'

Natalie nodded and wondered whether he made a habit of discussing her with his girlfriend behind her back. The thought made her feel slightly uneasy for some reason.

'I might as well tell you that I'll be sticking to Kane's side like glue, so if you think you can use the opportunity to wheedle yourself next to him, then you're in for a shock.'

Natalie moved towards the door, her body stiff with anger, but she still managed a smile. 'If you don't mind, I'm just about to lock up and go home.'

'He doesn't look twice at you, you know,' Anna said, flouncing out of the door towards the lift. Natalie followed her reluctantly, not having a great deal of choice.

'I never implied that he did,' she pointed out, stepping into the lift with the other woman and absent-mindedly staring at the buttons as the doors swished shut in front of them.

'I told him that you fancied him,' Anna continued and Natalie turned to face her, enraged.

'You did what?'

Anna threw her a sly look. 'Well, I thought it just as well to warn him. Men can be so stupid where women are concerned, and I didn't want him to find himself in any embarrassing situations.'

Natalie could have hit her. No wonder he had been so amused at the thought of her and Eric conducting a passionate affair; no wonder he had not believed a word of what she had said. Why should he? Anna had said her piece and hadn't Natalie herself responded to his lightweight kiss like some inexperienced teenager?

What a joke he must find it all.

'How good of you,' she said through gritted teeth.

'I hope you don't mind,' Anna said carelessly, pleased with the reaction which she had managed to stir.

'I don't really care.' The lift deposited them on to the ground floor and Natalie stepped out into the foyer with a feeling of intense relief. 'You can tell Kane Marshall anything you like,' she said quietly, in control of her emotions now, 'if it makes you feel better. But if I were you I would think very carefully about your relationship with him. I would say that if it was a solid one you wouldn't be looking over your shoulder continually, wondering whether you can trust him near other women.'

Anna gave her a look of spiteful hate. 'Of course I can trust him,' she hissed, but there was a shadow of doubt in her eyes. 'It's just that men are easily tempted.'

'Only if they want to be.' Natalie turned and began walking away, not daring to glance back behind her.

That unexpected meeting had left her feeling drained and depressed. She arrived back at her flat with that deflated, slightly sickened feeling still there in the pit of her stomach, and on impulse she went into her bedroom and began packing for the overnight stay, including an absolutely outrageous flame-red outfit which she had bought to celebrate her weight loss and which she had so far not actually screwed up the courage to wear.

Why should she fade away in greys and browns simply to keep a low profile? She threw in a pair of skin-tight flowered leggings which she would wear with a turquoise silk blouse on the Sunday morning, and by the time she had finished was actually feeling quite a bit better.

For all those years she had been an insignificant figure in an office, efficiently accomplishing her duties, overlooked by all of those women who trailed in on Kane's arm and then trailed back out again when he was finished with them. Now she would show the world at large that she might not be a staggering beauty, like Anna, but she could hold her own and be proud of the way she looked.

Eric must have sensed her defiance when he came to collect her the following afternoon because he immediately commented that there was something different about her. Natalie smiled and told him that the weather must have something to do with it, and it was true—the

sun was shining brilliantly and through the open window
the pleasant breeze made her want to shut her eyes and
drowse. She had made this trip to Kane's house several
times before, and she knew that it would take at least
two hours, and probably more like three if the traffic
proved unreliable.

His house, which he had inherited from his parents
when they emigrated to France, was in an idyllic little
village in Worcestershire—one of those charming places
which somehow managed to look endearingly quaint
without sliding into over-cute banality. It was oddly proportioned, quite small upstairs, but huge downstairs,
with enough room to entertain vast numbers of people
without a feeling of overcrowding. Which was probably
why his parents had bought it. Natalie knew that they
had entertained quite extensively before they emigrated.
In fact, she had been to their very last party before they
left the country and had thoroughly enjoyed it. She had
rather liked Kane's parents. They were intensely
charming, the sort of charm that brought a smile to your
lips.

As the car edged out of the London traffic and picked
up speed on the motorway Natalie relaxed and chatted
to Eric about the place, about the people who would be
there, and about what would be expected of her.

'Most girls would put their foot down at working on
weekends,' he said, glancing across at her with curiosity.

'It's become something of a bad habit,' Natalie told
him truthfully. 'I was very accommodating for a long
time; after all, I enjoyed the work and the money was
fantastic. Now he simply takes it for granted.'

'And you've never considered leaving?'

'Of course I have,' she protested; 'it's just that...'
Her voice dwindled off and she thought about what it

would be like to work somewhere without that constant excited tension in her at the thought that Kane would be around. Even in his absence she had not been able to shake him off because she had known that in due course he would reappear in her life.

'The money?' Eric prompted.

Natalie laughed and agreed vaguely, changing the subject. Recently, she had been thinking a great deal about all sorts of things, one of which was working with Kane. Sooner or later she would have to leave. When he had treated her only as a secretary, she had been able to feed her love from a distance, never questioning herself too much. But things were changing and matters which had previously only briefly popped into her head to pop back out again were looking up in a decidedly more threatening manner now.

It was just after six by the time they made it to the house. The car pulled up through the stone pillars, up the tree-shrouded avenue and into the courtyard.

Natalie had been there enough times to be fairly casual about the impressive edifice, but Eric let out a long whistle.

'Some house,' he said on a low, awe-struck tone.

Natalie gazed at it. It was a grand building, cream-coloured and set in acres of beautifully landscaped gardens.

'Why on earth does he live in London when he can move out here?' Eric asked in the same impressed voice, and Natalie laughed.

'Kane Marshall? In the country? On a full-time basis? I think he would go mad within a week. He once told me that he's the sort of person who needs stress to survive. He thrives on the fast pace of city life, and of course when he needs a rest he always has this to come to. In fact, you could say that he has the best of all possible worlds.'

She jumped out of the car and allowed Eric to carry her case up to the front door, which was opened by O'Leary after a couple of rings. He recognised Natalie instantly and gave her a coy smile. To Eric he directed a look of open suspicion which made her want to burst out laughing.

'I can't cope with all this to-ing and fro-ing at my age,' he told Natalie in an undertone, as he bustled around them in the hall, shutting the door with a huge clang. 'No sooner do we settle in the city than I get dragged up here to entertain the master's friends.'

Natalie stifled the grin at the thought of O'Leary entertaining.

'Has Mr Marshall arrived as yet?' she asked, noticing out of the corner of her eye Eric's reverential observation of the hallway with its original paintings and magnificent tapestry dominating the staircase wall.

'He has.' Kane's voice from behind her made her swing round to see him walking towards her, casually dressed in a pair of beige trousers with an olive-green shirt carelessly tucked into the waistband. He glanced across to Eric who had also turned at the sound of his voice, and Natalie wondered for a fleeting moment what was going through his head.

'I'll get back to the kitchen, then, shall I?' O'Leary muttered, shuffling off into the left-hand wing of the house.

Eric began to praise the house effusively, and Kane listened to him in polite silence, which irritated Natalie because she knew that it was deliberate, verging just slightly on the brink of rudeness, but when Eric flushed and paused in his eulogy Kane threw him that taste of urbane charm guaranteed to make you wonder whether you had misread his earlier coolness.

He caught Natalie's eye and she raised her eyebrow slightly, leaving him in no doubt that this little game was one that she could see through with no difficulty at all. She had seen it often enough in action and it usually succeeded in elevating Kane into a superior position.

He grinned at her and said, in a ultra-courteous voice, 'Shall I show you where you will be sleeping?'

They followed him up the vast staircase which curved around on to the first landing, and along the wide corridor to one of the doors on the right which he pushed open with a flourish.

'Here you go,' he said, then he turned to Natalie. 'O'Leary hasn't as yet made up the spare room for you. If you like, I can get him to do that now.' He lounged against the door-frame, his hands in his pockets, and surveyed her thoroughly, then his eyes flitted across to Eric, who was gazing around the room with evident admiration. 'Of course,' he murmured, teasingly, mock seriousness on his face, 'if you want to share this room...?'

He expected her to refuse. Vigorously. The horrified virgin who wouldn't dream of any such thing. She could hear the intonation in his voice, feel the expectancy hovering at the edge of his question, and she heard herself saying. 'Yes, I rather think I do.' There was a swift change of expression on his face and he stood upright, a sudden stillness about him which made her want to laugh out triumphantly. Except, she thought, appalled by her rashness, there was nothing to laugh about, was there?

'What the hell do you mean by that?' he asked in a low voice, as Eric moved across to the window to gaze outside, oblivious to what was going on. His green eyes devoured her, demanded a response, and she forced herself to answer lightly.

'I mean that there's no need for you to get O'Leary to clean the other spare room.' She turned to Eric and said in a louder voice, 'We'll both be fine in here.'

CHAPTER FIVE

KANE left the room without saying a word. As soon as the door clicked behind him, Natalie looked across to Eric with an expression of nervousness. It was one thing being defiant with Kane Marshall, but now she would have to suffer the consequences of this particular rebellion, and some instinct, which she could only assume was the prurient streak in her, balked at the prospect.

She had never, ever shared a room with a man before. Not in any circumstances. The thought of doing so now made her go hot with embarrassed anxiety. Not that she saw Eric as a threat. She didn't.

She smiled at him and cleared her throat. 'Here we are,' she said with a little cough. 'I...I really don't know what came over me just then.' She sighed heavily and sat on the bed, hoping that he wouldn't sit next to her.

'Nor do I,' Eric said. 'You're the last person I would have expected to rush into anything like this.'

Natalie stared at him, alarmed. 'Don't get the wrong idea, Eric,' she said quickly, in a high voice. 'I don't want...I didn't mean to let you think that...that...' Her voice trailed off and she looked at him hopefully to fill in the gaps in what she was trying to say.

'So why are we both here now?' he asked logically enough and Natalie shrugged her shoulders helplessly.

'Kane Marshall,' she said in a faltering voice, 'thinks that I'm...that I haven't got a clue about...anything. I suppose I just sort of rebelled on the spur of the moment.'

'You care that much about what he thinks of you?' Eric looked at her curiously and she flushed.

'Of course not! It's just that...'

He waited for her to finish but what more could she say without inadvertently telling him much more than she wanted him to know? She miserably trailed her finger along the ornate embroidered bedspread, and finally muttered, 'I don't want to sleep with you.'

Eric laughed ruefully. 'Thank you for being so blunt.'

Natalie looked at him, scarlet-faced. 'I'm sorry, I really don't mean to be offensive...'

Eric sighed and then said in an amicable enough voice, 'Go and get dressed, Natalie, before you tie yourself into even more knots. I get the message. You wanted to prove something to Kane Marshall, but that's it. Don't worry. At least you've stopped me from making a fool of myself.'

Was he angry? Natalie wondered, looking at him. He didn't appear to be too overwrought, but maybe he was clever at hiding his emotions. Whatever, there was no sense in dragging the whole discussion out. She had dug herself a pit and then willingly stepped into it, so all she could do now was make the best of the situation.

And Eric was as sympathetic as she could have wanted him to be, which would have been an insult if it wasn't instead such a huge relief. He made sure that the conversation was as impersonal as possible, scrupulously afforded her as much time as she wanted in the bathroom, and after a while some of that nervous panic began to leave her. She was more or less her usual calm self, at least on the surface, by the time she was dressed and ready to make her way downstairs.

Eric was still in the bathroom and rather than wait for him she made her own way to the kitchen, quickly looking over the food, which smelt delicious, listening to O'Leary's complaints about being too old for this sort of flash catering, and generally making sure that everything was going to run smoothly. It was the normal routine when she attended one of these weekend work parties, and she could handle it all with her eyes closed.

She was walking towards the lounge when she felt Kane's presence behind her. She had not heard him, but she knew that he was there because the hairs on the back on her neck stood on end and she got that slightly breathless, alert feeling that came over her whenever he was around.

She turned around to find him staring at her, lounging against the wall. He must have been in one of the downstairs rooms, and seen her as she had walked past. He was dressed formally in a deep grey, impeccably tailored suit, and Natalie thought that she had never seen anyone look quite so devastating in her life before.

Did he have any idea just how physically attractive he was? Probably. That didn't worry her, but what did worry her was what he might be thinking now about her, after what Anna had told him. Did he think that she was about to collapse in a dead faint at his enormous sex appeal?

'Hello,' she said, not moving towards him and making sure that her voice did not betray her emotions.

He grinned and remained where he was. Then, very deliberately, he let his eyes wander the length of her body, only slowly returning to meet her face, which was stony and disapproving.

Are you quite finished? she wanted to ask, but she dreaded the sort of cryptic, mocking answer that might meet her question, so instead she said calmly, 'Shall I wait for the guests in the lounge?'

'I've never seen you in that dress before.'

He moved towards her and Natalie felt her skin prickle with sudden, alarmed awareness.

'There are lots dresses you haven't seen me in before,' she murmured. She edged her way into the lounge, keenly conscious of him following her.

'I'm beginning to think that there's a whole lot about you that I don't know,' he said in a voice that sounded mildly accusing.

Natalie sat down and crossed her legs, noticing that in so doing a great deal of slender thigh was exposed. It made her feel uncomfortable, a hang-up from when she was overweight and inclined to hide rather than reveal.

'I do apologise,' she said with bland irony. 'I know you prefer the female sex to be one-dimensional.'

Kane laughed and poured them both a drink, placing hers on the coffee-table in front of her and then sitting on the sofa next to her, so close that she could feel the warmth emanating from his body.

'Whatever gave you that idea?' he asked silkily. 'I happen to know, and respect, quite a few highly intelligent women.'

'Oh, yes, that's true. I guess you just don't like them in your bed.'

She flushed at the stupidity of what she had just said and he laughed softly under his breath, whether at her discomfort or at her observation she didn't know.

'Sometimes I think that you're obsessed with my sex life,' he murmured.

'Not at all,' Natalie informed him evenly, remembering what Anna had told him and determined not to give him any leeway for thinking that she fancied him.

'I guess I just see a great deal of it first hand. After all, you've never exactly hidden the fact that you, you're...'

'Interested in women?' he prompted, amusement in his voice.

Natalie shrugged. 'Anyway,' she said, dragging the conversation back to a more manageable level, 'I bought this dress after I had lost some weight. It was a sort of present to myself.'

'And this is the first time that you're wearing it?' he asked.

She nodded and her breath caught in her throat as he reached out and trailed one finger along the neckline of the dress, following it to where it scooped down towards her breasts. Then she pulled back fiercely, her heart hammering in her chest.

'It flatters you,' he murmured in a voice that made her skin go warm, 'or maybe it's the other way around.'

She had to force herself to keep her body under control, and it made her angry. She didn't want to feel this way, dammit!

'Spare me your well-worn clichés,' she said tightly. 'Don't forget I know all those games you play with women.'

'Who's playing games?' he asked, his mouth curving into an amused smile. 'Or maybe you're one of those women who is incapable of accepting compliments at face value.'

Nothing you ever do is at face value, Natalie wanted to inform him. Did his sense of ego want him to prove that she was more attracted to him than she was to Eric? It wasn't a pleasant thought.

Her hand strayed to where his fingers had brushed against her skin. It still felt hot and prickly.

'If it was a genuine compliment, then thank you,' she muttered, not daring to meet those clever, assessing green eyes. 'It's just that I don't ever recall you having paid me any compliments in the past before. Except along the lines of work, of course.' And that suits me just fine, her voice implied. She tilted her chin defiantly to him and he raised one eyebrow in cynical amusement.

'Don't you? I recall a certain very attractive russet dress at a certain Christmas party...'

Colour stole along her cheeks until he could feel her face burning. She remembered the occasion as well. She had never forgotten it. She could recall every detail of what had happened between them, the music, the noise of the office workers, all slightly drunk, the secluded corner in which she had suddenly, alarmingly found herself alone with Kane, the huskiness in his voice when he told her that she looked beautiful.

Beautiful? Her? Every nuance of what she had felt then came flooding back to her now: the momentary thrill, quickly replaced by the agonising, bitter truth that there was nothing beautiful about her. She was overweight, hardly up to his standards in women. She had recoiled as though he had struck her, turning away so that he couldn't see the tears blurring her eyes. Of course he was drunk; he must have been. Drunk and not averse to leading on the secretary, in the absence of anyone else. Well, she wasn't going to be the face that greeted him when he awoke the following morning with a hangover.

She had left the room, running, and she had never worn that dress again. And from that day on she had made sure that she guarded her painful love tenaciously, fiercely, storing it safely behind that placid exterior.

It angered her now that another throw-away compliment could give her that same, wonderful, illicit thrill.

'Where's Anna?' she asked, changing the subject abruptly.

Kane gave her a sideways look from under his lashes. 'She arrived about an hour ago.' He paused. 'You would have seen her, but you were upstairs in your bedroom.' There was another pause while he continued to survey her. 'There was no need to share the room with him if you didn't want to, you know.'

'Why shouldn't I want to?' Natalie asked innocently.

'Lovers share bedrooms.' The outright blatancy of the remark made her gasp and he dropped his eyes. 'Are you his lover?' he asked in such a low voice that she wondered whether she had heard correctly.

'Would you mind pouring me another drink?' Natalie said in an over-loud voice. 'A glass of white wine please.'

'You haven't answered my question,' he repeated, his eyes flicking across to her face.

'It doesn't deserve an answer.'

He shrugged as though he didn't really care one way or another, but the lines of his face as he walked off to pour her drink were hard, even though when he next turned around to face her he was smiling.

She accepted the glass from him, and the conversation was dropped as the doorbell rang and the first of the guests began to arrive, along with Eric who apologised to her for taking slightly longer than necessary, but the technicality of arranging his bow-tie had proved more taxing than he had foreseen.

'If you'd been there, you could have helped me with it,' he said, and she had smiled drily at that piece of male chauvinism.

'I know nothing about bow-ties, and frankly I don't think I'm missing out on anything.'

The party turned out to be a good one. Kane had an instinctive ability to mix people together, knowing precisely which personalities would complement each other. There was a pleasant sound of voices filling the lounge, when the door opened and Anna made her entry.

Natalie had almost forgotten about the other woman. Now she, along with the other people in the room, women included, fell silent as she entered. Or rather, Natalie thought, made an entrance. Her long body was wrapped lovingly in a black dress that somehow managed to be modest, yet quite wanton in what it didn't reveal. No jewellery, except for a string of pearls and all that blonde hair upswept into a style that seemed perilously and attractively close to falling down.

Talking resumed, but she noticed that the men couldn't quite contain their surreptitious glances in Anna's direction. Including Eric, who had seemingly lost all interest in the business contact whom he was cultivating, and who, he had earlier confided in Natalie, might produce a lucrative source of work. So much for putting work before pleasure, she thought.

Anna's eyes flicked through the crowd and settled on Natalie. She smiled coyly, glancing back over her shoulder as she made her way towards Kane, and then proceeded to attach herself to his presence as if by invisible strings. At dinner, she sat next to him, smiling at appropriate intervals during the conversation which bounced between Kane on her right and the financial director of one of their important clients on the left.

Next to Natalie, Eric fought to hold on to what was being said to him, until Natalie finally said teasingly, 'Any chance I could have a bit of your attention?'

'Oh, sorry.' He faced her with a rueful smile. 'My mind was miles away.'

'Was it?' Natalie asked innocently. 'I thought it was at the other end of the table and sitting next to Kane Marshall.'

Eric flushed heavily. 'Was I being obvious?' he asked with a theatrical whisper.

'Just a little.' The thought amused her. Eric was safe, she thought fleetingly, because I'm not his sort at all. The impossibly beautiful are much more his cup of tea.

'I must be a glutton for punishment,' he sighed, concentrating on his dessert and doing it justice. 'She reminds me a lot of that model I was telling you about. The one who dumped me.'

Natalie looked thoughtfully to where Anna was sitting, her beautiful face averted towards Kane. Yes, men often were attracted to the same type of woman. Was that why she and Eric were so comfortable with each other? Because physically they were simply not to each other's taste?

She glanced at Eric. He was attractive enough, but in a bland way. How was it that his preferences lay in such exotic creatures as Anna?

The train of thought slipped to the back of her mind, as the plates were cleared away and fruit and cheese was brought out. In a while they would move into the lounge and have their after-dinner drinks. A few of the couples had been brought by taxi. Those who had committed themselves to driving back would eye the brandies and ports wistfully and blame their other halves for having all the fun.

Predictable but enjoyable enough, and Kane would have made a few business deals in the process. In the morning he would rattle off what had been achieved and she would type briefs of all of them while they were fresh in both their minds.

She looked at him out of the corner of her eye. He was chatting to one of his clients, laughing about something, a picture of ease. But she knew that, inside that head of his, his computer brain was ticking away, storing information. It was one of the things that made him so successful, she guessed. That amazing ability to retrieve information which most people would have relegated to the back of their mind and forgotten about. He could remember details of conversations from years back.

It was after midnight by the time the last of the guests had left. Kane had showed them to the door, with Anna clinging languorously to his arm, yawning prettily as the door shut. Even when she yawned she still managed to look delicate and beautiful. She could become a professional mud wrestler, Natalie thought sourly, and still manage to look sophisticated. No wonder Kane continued to toy with her. Would she be the one to finally catch the elusive fish?

They certainly made a good couple. Both tall, both commanding presences in their own way, and Anna's blonde good looks were the prefect foil to Kane's dark sensuality. And it had to be said that she had lasted a great deal longer than the rest of his playmates.

The thought of Kane marrying, settling down with a woman, made her stomach churn over.

'Shall I make a start on the clearing up?' she asked, stifling the sickening feeling.

Kane looked at her and shook his head. 'I've got a team of cleaners coming in tomorrow to take care of that.' He gave a crooked smile. 'You know O'Leary. He nearly had a heart attack at the thought of having to do it all on his own.'

Their eyes met in mutual, amused understanding and Anna looked at Natalie narrowly, her white hand tightening on Kane's arm. She didn't care for that at all. Natalie could see that immediately. The blonde woman yawned again, stretching with studied feline grace, and pouted at Kane.

'Shall we go to bed, darling?'

Eric's eyes were glued to the other woman and Natalie wondered tightly how someone could invest a simple sentence with such unspoken promise.

Kane nodded but his eyes were fixed on Natalie's face.

'Good idea,' he murmured, then he said softly and plainly for Natalie's benefit, 'I'm sure we're not the only ones who are eager to get to bed.' There was something hard and speculative in his eyes when he said that, and he looked away before he could read her response to his lazy insinuation.

He was hitting below the belt. What, Natalie wondered, could she do? Stand up and accuse him of what? Turning his sense of humour on her? It made her anger impotent, and she knew that that amused him even more.

She linked her arm through Eric's, relieved that his gaze was no longer plastered all over Anna, and preceded Kane and Anna up the staircase.

Upstairs, in the bedroom, Eric turned to her and said drily, 'There's an awful lot of innuendo behind your conversations with your boss. Or am I imagining it?'

'You're imagining it,' Natalie assured him flatly. She headed to the bathroom and quickly changed into her nightie, short, lacy and thoroughly inappropriate for sharing a bed with a platonic male friend.

Eric's pyjamas, striped and very sensible, were much more suited to the occasion. They eyed each other and Natalie said without preamble, 'I'll take the ground.'

The thought of actually sharing a bed with him, however safe he was, was enough to bring her out in a cold sweat. She had no option but to share the bedroom with him, but beds were for lovers. There was something way too intimate about that casual brushing of sleeping bodies, the feel of warm limbs against each other.

She grabbed the bedspread and began rigging something up on the ground. It wasn't that cold, so at least she would not have to contend with that particular problem.

'Oh, take the bed,' Eric grumbled good-naturedly.

'I got you into this,' Natalie said firmly. 'The least I can do is ensure that you're the one who has a good night's sleep.'

'And risk my reputation as being a man of honour?'

He began spreading the bedspread into what looked a bit like a makeshift sleeping-bag. Their fingers touched and Natalie pulled away instinctively.

'You're very attractive,' he murmured, looking at her seriously, and she felt a twinge of alarm.

'Eric, no,' she whispered. 'Don't make this difficult. We've been through all this.'

'We could go through it all again, but this time with a different conclusion,' he said hopefully, and she folded her arms across her breasts.

'Absolutely not!' Oh, God, she thought, please don't make him become difficult. She was not adept at handling difficult situations with men. She lacked the experience.

Eric grinned at her. 'Well, it was worth a try. Don't worry,' he continued, waving his white handkerchief when her expression didn't thaw, 'I'll be as good as gold on the ground.'

She relaxed a little, enough to flash him a watery smile. Good old Eric. If reason and fairness played any part in life, she and he would have found themselves besotted with each other. If reason and fairness played any part in life, she would have listened to her head a long time ago and left the Marshall Corporation. She would have found a job working for a Mr Average, in an average company, and she would have eventually settled down with an averagely pleasant person. Like herself.

She slipped into bed, letting the darkness wrap itself around her while the thoughts played around in her mind, swooping and teasing until she finally fell asleep.

Eric was already up by the time she next opened her eyes. She could hear him singing away in the bathroom. He had neatly refolded the bedspread and not quite so neatly dumped the pillows back on the bed. She closed her eyes and relaxed on the bed, feeling pleasantly lazy.

She didn't hear the door open at all. In fact, the first she knew of Kane's presence in her bedroom was when he spoke, then her eyes flew open and she stared at him in alarm.

'What are you doing here? Why didn't you knock?'

'I did knock.' He was looking around the room, his eyes taking in everything, until they resettled on her face. 'Slept well?' There was a hardness around his mouth, even though his tone was bantering. Was he annoyed about something? she wondered. It was only slightly after eight o'clock, so he could hardly make a song and dance about not getting up early enough to start work. Anyway, there was no excuse for him barging into her bedroom. He had never done that before. She had hitched the duvet cover up to her neck and she sat up.

'Very strait-laced,' Kane commented. His eyes flicked across to the bathroom. 'I can't imagine why you're bothering. Not when your lover is in the bathroom.'

'What are you doing here?' she repeated. 'If you've come to fetch me to begin work, I'll be down in about half an hour.' She glanced across at the bathroom door. 'As soon as Eric emerges.'

He moved across to the bed and sat on the edge of it. Natalie watched him in growing dismay.

'And when is that likely to be?' Kane asked softly.

Natalie shook her head. 'I have no idea. He seems to like spending a long time in the bathroom.'

'Without you? I'm surprised.'

Natalie's heart gave a quick skip. Dismay was rapidly growing into panic.

'And I'm surprised you're not with Anna,' she responded as tartly as she could.

'Are you? Perhaps that's because she's beginning to bore me slightly.'

Natalie looked down, overcome by the swift stab of delight that single sentence brought her, and then hating herself for being so foolish.

'I'm sorry,' she lied.

He gave a short laugh. 'Why? It's hardly the end of the world. Women come and go.'

Natalie didn't say anything. Did he think that she hadn't noticed that a long time ago?

'Only with you,' she murmured. He reached forward, leaning above her, his hands on either side of her body, trapping her.

'I prefer not to let my relationships with women pall. But you know that, don't you? You know a lot about me, don't you?' His voice was soft and vaguely menacing. 'More than I apparently know about you. For instance, I have to admit I half expected to find bedlinen on the floor and only half the bed slept in.'

'I'm so sorry to have disappointed you, in that case.' Why deprive herself the chance of maintaining some control? Let him believe the worst; wasn't it better than letting him glimpse the truth?

'You haven't disappointed me,' he said tersely, 'merely surprised me. But then you always have.'

That made her look at him. What did he mean by that?

'So tell me,' he carried on relentlessly, 'are the two of you serious?'

When she shrugged, he stretched out one hand, curling his fingers in her hair so that she was forced to look at him. Panic was now making her breathing difficult and uneven.

'Does he turn you on?' He glanced quickly at the bathroom door, as if to reassure himself of something, then he said roughly, 'Does he?'

'That's none of your business,' she gasped.

'You're right, it isn't.' He half smiled at her, a charming, persuasive smile that should have made her fly out of the room and run as fast as her legs could take her, but which instead rooted her to the spot, mesmerised.

'There's always one way of finding out,' he murmured, and Natalie had no need to ask what it was, because it clicked the moment he leaned towards her, parting her lips with restless urgency. He sighed against her mouth and raised his hand to her head, cupping her neck. Natalie closed her eyes and gave in to the driving hunger that had been a part of her for so long. Her mouth moved feverishly against his, their tongues intermingling with electric intimacy. The sensations gripping her were quite different from anything she had ever experienced before.

How could she have ever entertained the idea of becoming involved with Eric? Or with anyone else for that matter? She would never be able to escape Kane's clutches. Without realising it, he had made her a prisoner of her own love.

The force of his kiss had pushed her back against the pillow, dislodging the duvet cover to reveal the lacy femininity of her nightdress. With Eric, she had been quite unaware of its sensual allure. She might just as well have been wearing a pair of thick flannelette pyjamas.

With Kane, though, it was different. He looked at her hungrily, and she could feel his eyes burning her, making her want to squirm with agonising excitement. And he was as excited as she was. She could see it in his quick breathing, and in the drowsy, feverish glow in his eyes.

He bent over to kiss her neck, and as she arched back to accommodate him his hand found the full swell of her breast. He caressed it, his fingers playing with the hardened peaks of her nipples through the lace.

'This is madness,' Natalie groaned unevenly. 'Eric . . .'

'Is still lustily singing in the bathroom.' His mouth closed over hers once again, as she made a small movement to push him away, and her hands curled helplessly around him. He moved lower to cover her breast with his mouth, dampening the lace so that it clung to her form, outlining her nipple, which was hard and aching and pushing through one of the gaps in the delicate material. He nibbled against it, then with a deft movement he dislodged the slender strap from her shoulder and scooped out her breast. Natalie watched his dark head lowered over it and yielded to his heated onslaught.

It was only when he raised his head to look at her that the first drop of sanity began to return. She heard it as clearly as he did: the silence in the bathroom. Eric was no longer singing.

With a desperate movement, she wriggled free into a less compromising situation, tugging back on her nightie, while Kane sat up on the bed and carelessly ran his fingers through his hair. He didn't look as though he cared one way or the other whether Eric caught them at anything.

He might not care, Natalie thought, but I certainly do.

'A little late for pursed lips, don't you think?' Kane commented harshly, standing up but continuing to stare at her. 'You weren't exactly pushing me away a moment ago.'

Natalie struggled to find some reasonable explanation for her behaviour, some excuse that she could hurl at him that might make it all forgivable, but she couldn't think of a single thing. She could still feel her skin tingling from where he had touched it, and the one thought that kept revolving in her head was that she must have been insane.

'You'd better go,' she said stiffly, and Kane looked at her with freezing disdain.

'Does Eric know exactly what sort of person you are?' he asked with a cool, assessing smile.

'What do you mean?'

'Do I have to spell it out in black and white?' His voice was rapid and hard and every word was aimed to wound. 'You've shared your bed with Eric, but you don't exactly mind sharing it with me as well, do you?'

'That's not true!'

'Isn't it?' He stuck his hands in his pockets and stared at her coldly. 'Dear me, maybe I misread the obvious. Did you share your bed with Eric?'

'That's none of your business...!'

'I rest my case.'

They stared at each other in thick silence, then Natalie felt the stirrings of anger. Just who did Kane Marshall think he was? The patron saint of good behaviour? Oh, he didn't mind standing there and making his insinuations, but he wasn't exactly making them from a position of moral superiority, was he?

'You would rest your case,' she said bitterly. 'You've reached your conclusions and that's the end of the story as far as you're concerned. Not,' she added forcefully, 'that I have any intention of defending myself anyway——'

'Very wise, considering you would find that a little on the difficult side...'

She ignored his interruption. 'I would just like to ask just who the hell you think you are, anyway! You with your women. So what if I choose to sleep with one man, or a thousand men for that matter? It would only be on a par with you!'

His face reddened but he didn't take his eyes off her. 'Don't you dare lecture to me on my love life,' he grated.

'Then don't lecture to me on mine!' She was clinging to her duvet cover and her knuckles were white. Her body was burning all over, with rage and that dreadful, impotent feeling of having been unjustly condemned— and with the awful knowledge that she had allowed herself to be humiliated for the stupidest of reasons— she had wanted to taste him, to feel him after waiting for so many years.

'You'd better leave,' she told him.

'Gladly,' he murmured, turning and walking out without a backward glance.

As the door shut quietly behind him, the one leading to the bathroom opened and Eric emerged, pink and washed.

'Are you all right?' he frowned. 'I thought I heard voices.'

'You did.' Natalie smiled at him brightly. 'It was just Kane. He wanted to tell me what time to start this morning.'

Eric looked dubiously at her. 'Are you sure that was all?'

'Of course!' She laughed airily even though her throat felt dry and painful. 'What else? You seem to forget, I'm not Anna. I'm his secretary.'

Please, she thought desperately, never let me forget that again.

CHAPTER SIX

KANE kept Natalie busy for the remainder of the week. As fast as one pile of work was reduced, another one swelled to take its place, and on top of that she had to find the time to keep on top of her newly appointed accounts.

For the first time since she had been working there she felt an absurd urge to be reassured that she could handle everything, that her promotion had not been a huge mistake, but asking Kane for that kind of assurance was out of the question. Self-doubt was something he had not been afflicted with. She knew that he would treat it in other people with that barely concealed impatience that was more effective than outright irritation.

Besides, she didn't want to broach anything remotely personal with him. She just wanted to put her head down and get on with her work, and if she cracked under the strain of it, then she would simply glue the pieces back together in the privacy of her flat, and carry on.

Eric was slightly put out that he could not see her. He had quite quickly, too quickly, grown accustomed to her compliance in falling in with his plans. She patiently explained that she was working twelve-hour days, but he still grumbled.

'He can't work you like that. You shouldn't put up with it! The man's a slave-driver.'

'What do you suggest?' Natalie had asked, smiling down the telephone receiver. 'A sit-down strike? Work to rule?'

'Why not?'

'Because chances are he would decide that I wasn't worth the bother. I'd find myself conducting my sit-down strike in one corner of the room while he introduced my replacement in the other.'

What she couldn't explain was that she enjoyed working late. When Kane was focused on work to the exclusion of everything else, there was a powerful cama-raderie between them. They could communicate almost without talking. It was dangerous from her point of view, but it still gave her a high, made her feel vibrantly alive and tuned in to him.

On the Friday, she was almost tempted to give in to Eric's invitation to dinner. Kane was in Paris for a series of meetings and was not going to be back. In the end, a dogged determination to clear her desk made her refuse, and she remained in the office until after seven o'clock, wearily struggling back to her flat for a light supper of salad and cheese. She felt physically exhausted, but pleasantly so. She had not had much time to think during the week. Now, she sat in front of the television, with her plate on her lap, and all those thoughts which had taken a back seat rose from the shadows and started to nibble away at her consciousness.

What had happened in the bedroom five days ago still made her body burn. She could remember in vivid and agonising detail every touch of his hand, the feel of his lips exploring her mouth and breasts, the heat from his body making hers tremble with desire.

Of course she had known that she was in love with him. She had known that for a long time. She was no fool, and she had never tried to hide that inescapable fact from herself. But what she had not known was the depth of reaction that physical contact with him would stir in her. Because she had controlled her love for years, living with it but never letting it escape from the narrow confines in which she nurtured it, she had always assumed that everything was under control.

Nothing could have prepared her for what she had felt when Kane had kissed her, when he had touched her in places that had never been touched before. Was it all the harder to bear because she was so inexperienced? Would she have been able to cope if she had had a fraction of the worldliness that most girls her age possessed?

She stared vacantly at the television and the image of Kane in her mind was so powerful that he could just as well have been standing in front of her. What a big joke it must have been for him, proving that he could stoke the fires burning underneath that cool, controlled face of hers.

Was that why he had come into the bedroom? Hoping that Eric would not be around? Or was it just an opportunity which he had seized, a spot of early morning amusement?

Whatever, the consequences remained the same. She had reacted to him like a gauche schoolgirl and he had laughingly played on her response as skilfully as a musician playing his instrument. The fact that Eric's presence in the bathroom had not deterred him only showed the contempt in which he held all her declarations about caring about Eric, about being passionate about him.

She picked at her salad and tried to focus on the television screen, but it was difficult. In the end she dumped her plate in the kitchen and retrieved her book from where it was lying on the table next to her bed.

She was re-reading chapter three for the fourth time when the doorbell rang. One short, sharp buzz and she rose to her feet crossly. She was not in the mood for company this evening. It was late, she looked a mess in her faded jeans and faded T-shirt, and, besides, she knew the identity of her caller. Eric. Who else could it be?

Well, she would have to have a strong chat to him if he thought that he could turn up at her flat any old time. She didn't want that kind of relationship with him. Not now. Maybe not ever. Friends or no friends. She pulled open the door with a sigh and her eyes widened at the figure standing in front of her.

'What are you doing here?' In all these years, Kane had never before come to see her at her flat. She had been adamant about that one thing—there was no way that she would ever let him intrude into her private territory, even if it was only for the purposes of work. She didn't object to working at his place, if absolutely necessary, but that was it.

Now she stared at him, aghast. Had he come here straight from the airport? It looked like it. He was still in his suit, although the jacket had been discarded as had the tie, and the sleeves of the white shirt had been carelessly rolled to the elbow, exposing the firm brown flesh of his arms, with their sprinkling of dark hair.

'Aren't you going to let me in?' Kane asked drily.

Natalie reluctantly stepped aside and watched while he walked into her flat, his tall, powerful body filling it with his charisma. She stayed by the door, one hand still on the doorknob, praying that what he had come for would only take five minutes.

There was no point in trying to hustle him out because that would only encourage him to stay longer. All the same, she couldn't resist repeating her question of what he was doing in her flat. At this hour. Without an invitation. She phrased her question as tactfully as she could, but his eyebrows shot up in feigned surprise and she met his eyes evenly.

'Do I take it that you'd rather I was not here at all?'

Natalie didn't say anything and he read her silence for agreement.

'You weren't expecting any other company, were you?' They both knew who he meant by company and she shook her head.

'I only just got back here about an hour ago myself,' she confessed after a while. 'I decided to work late tonight and clear the backlog.'

'What a dedicated little thing you are.' He prowled around the room, and then sat down on the sofa, picking up her book and twirling it around in his hand, as if trying to discover something about her from her taste in literature.

Reluctantly Natalie shut the door and moved into the room. She didn't want this at all, but he could be totally insensitive if it suited him, and clearly he had no intention of leaving just yet, however pointedly she stood by the door tapping her foot and glaring at her watch.

'Aren't you going to offer me anything to eat or drink?' He smiled at her persuasively, his green eyes warm and teasing.

'There's nothing in the fridge to eat,' Natalie informed him. 'I can make you a cup of coffee if you like.'

'Please don't put yourself out. I wouldn't want you to collapse from the effort,' Kane drawled, but his eyes were sharp with amusement. He cocked his head to one side, waiting for her retort, and Natalie walked off into the kitchen, thankful for the privacy to get her thoughts together.

What was he doing here? He was here for a reason, and since his arms were not burdened under the weight of files she could only assume that it wasn't to do with work.

The haziness of the alternative made her tremble with apprehension. She returned to the lounge and handed him his cup of coffee, then retired to the furthest chair away from him, and surveyed him from under her lashes, troubled.

'What are you doing here?' she asked finally.

'I merely came to say thank you for all the long hours you put in this past week.' He looked at her, offended, but she knew better than to think that he really cared one way or another what she thought of him.

'That's quite all right,' she said with an optimistic glance at the door. 'Although there was no need to come over here,' she consulted her watch, 'at nine-thirty to tell me.'

'I was tired and hungry and I wanted someone to chat to,' Kane said with a hint of irritation in his voice.

The implication was there that any other woman would have been flattered at his sudden appearance on her doorstep, tired and hungry and in need of a chat.

'How did the meetings go?' she asked, seeing with a frown that switching the conversation on to work had not met with his approval. But what did he expect? Did he subconsciously think, from her reaction to him, that she was amenable to him whenever he chose?

He clicked his tongue impatiently and briefly told her what had been decided at the meetings. Natalie listened with interest. This aggressive, manipulative skill in

dealing with other people on a work level never failed
to intrigue her. She had never known anyone who could
handle himself with such self-assured ease, and looking
at him in action was always a treat.

'I didn't come here to talk about work,' he said,
rubbing his eyes and relaxing back on the sofa. Natalie
studied his reclining figure with a sense of fascinated
alarm, as if any minute now he would spring into action
and she would have to run for her life.

'What did you come to talk about?'

He shrugged and looked at her from under his lashes.
'Anything you'd like to, provided it has nothing to do
with work.'

Natalie's heart skipped a beat and then went into
overdrive. Something in that dark, intimate gaze made
the blood rush to her head, made her all too aware that
they were alone together. This time there was no Eric
singing in the bathroom to remind them that reality was
only a hair's breadth away.

Then she laughed at herself. Where was she letting her
imagination lead her?

'Don't you have a girlfriend to fulfil those needs?'

He shot her a lazy smile. 'What needs in particular
are you referring to?'

The sudden silence was deafening.

'You know what I mean,' Natalie said on an angry
note. He was playing games with her. Maybe the delightful Anna wasn't around. Whatever the reason, she
didn't see why she had to put up with him in her flat,
confusing her for his own benefit.

'Anna doesn't listen the way that you do. Besides,
she's—what shall I say?—getting a little demanding.'

'I see.' So she was on her way out. After all that possessiveness, those threats, she was on her way out whether

she liked it or not. Kane could be quite ruthless in his personal life.

'She's beginning to insinuate that there might be more to life than sex.'

Natalie suspected that he was being deliberately provocative in his choice of words, but his face was perfectly serious.

'Silly Anna,' she said. 'She can't know you very well.'

'But you do, don't you?' Kane said softly, and Natalie looked across the room at him, startled. All of a sudden panic gripped her by the throat, making her sick.

'I'll get you another cup of coffee,' she mumbled, standing up and reaching for his mug on the coffee-table, half afraid that he would stretch out and grab her by the wrist.

But he didn't, and she walked into the kitchen, only aware that he was following when she felt his presence by the doorway.

'Why do women think that marriage is the inevitable conclusion to a relationship?' he asked, leaning against the door-frame and surveying her.

When it comes to you, Natalie felt like saying, I have no idea. Marriage and Kane Marshall seemed about as compatible as fire and water. At least I never entertained that idea, she thought; at least I knew where to draw the line. I might have been a fool to fall in love with him, but I wasn't so stupid as to imagine that he would look at me twice, or even if he did that it would lead to anything at all. He was a catch, though. One of those big fish that every angler wanted on the end of her line.

'Do you think that marriage is the inevitable conclusion to a relationship?' he asked curiously.

Natalie handed him his mug and tried to edge her way past him, but he stretched out one arm, barring her exit, forcing her to stare up at him.

A sudden brainwave hit her. 'Yes,' she said emphatically, feeling a swift moment of triumphant satisfaction at her own cleverness. 'Yes, as a matter of fact, I do. What's the point of getting to know someone if at the end of the day all you do is part company? What's the point? No, for me, it's marriage, and children, the lot.' She smiled, totally relaxed now that she had decided on this defensive action. If it was one thing to scare off Kane Marshall, it was a woman with commitment on her mind, and she badly wanted to scare him off right now. She didn't care for him in her flat, she didn't care for the way he had looked at her in the lounge, and she certainly didn't care for the heady sensations that had been washing over her from the very moment he had entered the place.

'And solid Eric promises all those things?' His mouth twisted cynically and her eyes clashed with his defensively, but she didn't reply. Lying on that scale would have been a bit too blatant.

He took her silence for agreement. 'I knew it was on the cards,' he muttered. 'Didn't I ask you whether a man was behind all that?' He gestured to her and Natalie choked back her automatic response to deny it.

'Everyone's different,' she said truthfully, thinking aloud. 'Some people, like you, don't want commitment. You like your freedom . . .'

'Damn right,' he bit out, as though she had been attacking him. 'What's wrong with that?' He gave her a dark, brooding look. 'And I thought that you agreed with me.'

'Me?' Natalie looked at him in surprise. 'Whatever gave you that idea?'

'You never thought anything of my succession of females. Not that you said, anyway.'

Natalie shrugged. 'It was none of my business.' She stared down at her fingers, twining them together on her lap. It was none of her business, that was true enough, but that had never stopped her from hurting every time she knew that there was a new woman on the scene, did it? That had never stopped her fertile mind from throwing up all sorts of images of Kane and his latest conquest in bed together, had it?

'The perfect secretary,' Kane grated cynically, 'mind set only on work. No opinions on anything else. Or do you keep it all so well hidden?'

He stood up and prowled around the room, finally standing by the bay window and staring outside, his hands in his pockets.

'I had no idea that I was paid to voice my opinions,' she said.

'You're voicing them now.' He looked around at her, and her heart fluttered uneasily in her chest. 'I like that. Why don't you do it more often? Are you scared of me? No, don't answer that; I know you're not. Even when you don't say a word I know it's not because you're scared of my response. Dammit, most women are usually so awed by money and power. It makes them compliant. Who the hell wants compliance?'

'Did you come here to pick a fight with me?'

'Of course not. You know why I came.' He raked his fingers through his hair and stared at her. 'I wanted company. And you're the most intelligent female company I know.'

That would be a compliment, Natalie thought sadly, except you don't really like intelligent women, do you? Not in large doses at any rate. Despite what you sometimes would have me believe.

'Aren't you going to react to that?' he asked softly, moving closer to where she was sitting. Natalie felt her body tense. Something in the atmosphere had changed very subtly between them.

'Should I?'

'Well, most normal women would be flattered by a compliment.'

'Thank you,' she said obediently, 'I'm flattered.'

His lips twisted in a mocking smile. 'Very sincere,' he murmured, moving still closer until he was looming over her, making her break out in nervous perspiration. Did he know what he was doing to her? she wondered.

'I'm sorry,' Natalie said tartly, 'perhaps I should tremble in gratitude that the great Kane Marshall has deigned to pay me a compliment.'

'That tongue of yours,' he replied, his eyes hard. 'I can't imagine what brought me here. It certainly isn't a relaxing experience.'

'You know where the door is,' she muttered, not loudly enough for him to hear, although he tried to.

The conversation, she knew, was rapidly getting out of hand. It was late, they were both away from the security of a working environment, and a lot could be said that would later be regretted. She knew that. She worked for him after all. However much she didn't like admitting it, there was a limit to what she ought to say to him, because tomorrow was another day.

'What I really came to say,' he muttered, 'was this. Does solid Eric know that you're attracted to me?'

Natalie's mouth fell open.

'Well, does he?' Kane prompted coolly. 'I've spent some time thinking about what happened last Sunday and I've come to the conclusion that it's a bit unfair of you to conduct a relationship with a man to whom you can't possibly be attracted.' Every word made her body go colder until she felt as though any moment her teeth would begin chattering.

'You never said anything to me at work,' she breathed, at a loss for anything else to say, and he gave a short laugh.

'I didn't think work was exactly a fitting environment for observations of that nature.' He looked away and a dark flush crept up his face. 'Answer me—does he? Does he know how you feel about me?'

Natalie stood up abruptly, making no attempt to disguise her shaking hands.

'Out!' she said in a high voice. 'Get out of my flat!'

He didn't budge, and she raised her hand in a fit of angry, humiliated rage, sweeping it across his face, recoiling from the stinging contact of flesh against flesh. A red mark immediately appeared on his cheek. He reached out and snatched her hand by the wrist, twisting it and pulling her towards him so that she was on tiptoe, unable to wriggle because the slightest movement made her trapped hand go hot with pain.

'Truth a little painful for you, Miss Robins?' he hissed. 'Anna told me that you were attracted to me, but I didn't believe her. I thought it was her imagination getting way out of control, but she was right, wasn't she? You are attracted to me, and what I want to know is what you're going to do about it.'

'You don't know what you're talking about,' Natalie whispered. Her entire body felt as though any minute it would burst into flame. She was hot with embarrassment, she didn't know where to look and much as she wanted to cover her ears with her hands, to scream at him to shut up, what good would it do? It wouldn't stop him from knowing the awful truth. The only saving grace was that at least he didn't know the depth of her attraction.

'Oh, yes, you do. When you lay in my arms, I could feel your whole body melting, urging me on to take you.'

'I don't want to hear this.'

'I'm sure you don't. I'm sure you'd like to run away from the truth as fast as your legs can take you, and pretend that what you want is a life of marriage, two children, one dog and a goldfish, but don't you think that's a bit unfair on yourself? Why pretend? You'll never be able to settle for second best. It's not in your nature. You're too stubborn to just make do.'

'How dare you come into my flat and…and…?' Her sentence spluttered to a standstill and she glared at him, her eyes bright with unshed tears of anger.

'And force you to face a few hard facts?'

'So I'm attracted to you,' she shouted. 'All right, I admit it, I'm attracted to you, but that doesn't mean anything!' They were the bitterest words she had ever spoken and she bent her head, defeated, rather than witness the flare of triumph in his eyes.

'Doesn't it?' He released her hand and she snatched it away, massaging it until circulation resumed. She only wished that she could take herself off to some other part of the room, to escape the claustrophobic weight of his masculinity, but her legs remained rooted to the spot.

'Sex isn't the most important thing in the world,' she said shakily. What she wanted to say was that love was far more important than sex, but the mere thought of introducing that word into the conversation made her go cold. No, he was too shrewd for his own good, and it wouldn't do to let him have any opportunity to think that what she felt for him extended beyond physical attraction.

'Of course it isn't,' he agreed roughly, 'but it's nice, though, isn't it?' He bend downwards and his lips found hers with a hot urgency that made her pull back in alarm and fright.

His arms met around her, pulling her back against him so that she was pressed to his body, and could feel his hard arousal.

'I really think you ought to go,' she said weakly. 'It's very late and I... I have to be up early in the morning for work.'

'Tomorrow's Saturday,' he reminded her.

'I meant I must be up early for... I have an appointment.'

'Why are you so afraid?'

'I'm not afraid!' she wailed, but she was. Desperately afraid. All these years she had been able to hold her emotions in check because they had never been put to the test. Now she feared that her love for him would be her final weakness. His hand moved to the nape of her neck, his fingers intermingling in her hair, tugging her head gently back so that she had to meet his stare.

This time his mouth met hers with coaxing sweetness. He was no longer demanding a response, he was merely enticing her with a temptation too powerful to resist. He parted her lips with his, and she felt the warmth of his tongue flicking in her mouth, sending shooting currents down her back.

'Don't tell me you don't know,' he murmured huskily. 'I've thought about this all week. Why do you think I had to come over here?'

He lifted her off her feet in one deft movement and carried her towards the general direction of the bedroom, kicking open doors until he found it. Then he kicked shut the door and gently deposited her on the bed.

Natalie lay down, her eyes half closed, and knew that she would never forgive herself if she gave in to this piece of insanity. She meant nothing to him but an available body, one which he was curious to discover. But she had worked for him for years. She knew his track record. He tired easily, and she knew that if he slept with her he would tire even more quickly than usual. After all, she was not in the class of his other women. She had made the most of herself, but she was still an ordinary girl. Too many cream cakes and she would become that plump little thing that no one had ever noticed.

'What are you thinking?' he asked, lying down next to her.

'We shouldn't be doing this,' she said, hearing the feebleness in her own ears and wishing desperately that she could summon up the good sense to do something about it.

'We're attracted to each other, so why not?' He kissed her cheeks, tiny feathery kisses that made her shudder in response and she twisted round to face him. The blood was racing through her veins, making her giddy. Was that why she couldn't seem to shed her inertia? When he kissed her lips, she sighed and returned the kiss, hesitantly at first, then hungrily as she gave in to the abandon raging through her.

He reached under her T-shirt, finding her bare skin and stroking it in long, even movements. Natalie groaned and lay flat on the bed. She couldn't stop now. She wanted him too badly for common sense to have any room. Her breasts were aching to feel his touch, and when his hand found them she wriggled with ecstasy. He rubbed the nub of her nipple, then pulled the T-shirt up and over her head.

It still wasn't too late to stop, she knew that. He would go if she insisted, but she didn't insist. She watched, fascinated, as he unbuttoned his shirt, exposing the muscled breadth of his chest, with its dark hair tapering below his navel into the waistband of his trousers. She had never seen a naked man before. When he undressed, she stared, knowing that he was amused by the expression on her face.

'You look amazed,' he whispered, settling next to her and guiding her hand to his maleness.

'I am.' She gulped and then burst out, 'I've never...'

'Never?' His face was serious. 'But what about Eric?'

'He never...we never...' Words failed her and she lapsed into embarrassed silence, wondering whether he would find her virginity a complete turn-off. She did. She thought it was ridiculous in this day and age, but some frustrating uprightness had stood in the way of her ever sleeping with a man without love.

'To be your first,' he moaned into her ear, and she realised that her virginity was anything but a turn-off for him.

He unzipped her jeans and slid his hand underneath, running it over the flat contours of her stomach, teasing her until she felt as if she was going to dissolve in desire. She traced her finger over her breast, tempting him in turn, satisfied when he could no longer resist and bent his head to suckle on one pink peak. She arched back, thrusting her breast into his mouth, loving the feel of his moist lips around it while his tongue darted across the nipple.

With his hand he helped her wriggle free of her jeans so that she was left in her lacy underwear, then he caressed her thighs, his fingers finally working their way under her briefs to arouse her to a pitch of passion which she was finding difficult to control. He was taking his time, though, and for that she was grateful. He knew that she was inexperienced and every touch was gentle as he explored her body.

He kissed her stomach, and she felt her breathing become difficult as his head moved lower, he gently eased her briefs from her, and his lips caressed her most intimate parts with a tender persuasiveness that made her gasp with pleasure. She parted her legs to accommodate him, her body jerking to the rhythm he was setting, until she pleaded with him to satisfy her completely.

There was a short, sharp pain as he thrust into her, then only mounting bliss as he moved deep inside. He bent down to kiss her lips with fierce hunger and under the palms of her hands she could feel his back damp with perspiration. She closed her eyes and let sensation sweep her away. How could she think that she could ever have made love with anyone else? For her it had been an unbelievable experience.

Later, as they lay next to each other on the bed, her head nestled in the crook of his arm, she wondered where they would go from here. What happened in situations like these? Was there some blueprint for behaviour?

He kissed her ear, tucking her hair carefully behind the lobe and whispered that she was beautiful.

If only she could believe it. 'Hardly,' she murmured, blushing, and as if to assure her that he was telling the truth he led her hand to his arousal as it once again throbbed into life.

Natalie wished that this would never end. Reason was so cold and harsh, but already, even while she enjoyed the heights of pleasure to which he was taking her, it was establishing itself.

It was telling her that regret was only a short step away.

CHAPTER SEVEN

THINGS always looked different in the cold light of day. Nightmares faded, depression lifted, hope sprang into life.

Natalie stared at the first light of dawn through the crack in the curtains and thought that she couldn't have been more miserable if she had tried. She looked down to where Kane was still sleeping, his face oddly vulnerable in repose, and closed her eyes. Memories of their lovemaking flooded through her mind, making her body tingle. So what was she going to do now? She had succumbed to temptation, unable to resist what he was offering her, and she knew that a price had to be paid.

She shifted as quietly as she could to slip out of the bed and his hand flicked out, catching her by the wrist, making her start. Had he known that she had been staring at him?

'Going somewhere?' he asked lazily, looking at her with a possessive intimacy that made her body burn.

Natalie cleared her throat. This situation would have to be handled delicately. There was no sense in weeping and wailing and tearing her hair out over what she had done. On the other hand, she knew with profound sadness that she could not be yet one more woman in his life, a dalliance that he would grow tired of soon enough and discard when she had outgrown her novelty value.

120

'I thought I might make us some coffee,' she murmured, and he picked up his watch from the side of the bed.

'At five-thirty in the morning?' His eyes focused with drowsy sexiness on her face. 'Are you in the habit of getting up this early?'

Natalie laughed uncomfortably. 'I'm not used to sharing my bed with anyone, I suppose.'

He pulled her towards him and there was a glimmer of satisfaction in his eyes. 'I know. I like that. It turns me on.' He found her mouth with his, and she felt her treacherous body stir into life once again. Very gently, she disengaged herself from his arms, even though every fibre of her being was screaming out for her to abandon her pointless principles and enjoy what he could give her for as long as he could give it.

'Coffee?' she reminded him, with a trace of desperation in her voice. 'Or tea?'

Kane lay back down, his hands behind his head, and looked at her from under his lashes. 'I'd rather have you,' he drawled and a wash of hectic colour flooded her cheeks.

She made herself remember that all these were old lines for him, clichés that he rattled out for every woman who shared his bed. Because his voice was slightly uneven, because he sounded sincere, didn't mean a thing.

'I'll be back in a moment.' She stood up, horribly conscious of her nudity, and of his green eyes surveying her lingeringly. She slipped on her bathrobe and hurried off to the kitchen, feverishly making them both some coffee and trying to work out what on earth she was going to do now. She couldn't afford to spend much more time with him. She couldn't afford to let his charm and sheer animal sex appeal make her forget her resolutions.

He was sitting up when she returned to the bedroom.

'What is it?' he said abruptly, as she perched on the chair by the dressing-table, with her mug cradled in her hands.

Natalie gave him a blank look. 'What's what?'

'Don't play games with me, Natalie,' he said sharply, 'Something's wrong. Why else would you be sitting over there with that cup of coffee between your hands, like some damned schoolmistress about to discipline an unsuspecting pupil?'

'Well, if you must know...' She sought for the right phrase, sensing his mounting anger with dismay. 'If you must know...' She took a deep breath and plunged on. 'About last night—it should never have happened. I don't know what came over me.'

'Lust,' Kane said tightly. He stood up, throwing the covers back, and Natalie averted her eyes. 'Look at me,' he commanded. 'You've touched this naked body, so looking away is rather like shutting the door after the proverbial horse has bolted, isn't it?'

'I don't expect you to understand...'

He moved towards her so quickly that she barely had time to catch her breath, and pulled her to her feet, yanking her towards him, his face thrust into her own.

'I damn well understand,' he bit out, 'you've spent a lifetime denying that desire can be any part of your life, and you're ashamed of what happened between us.'

'I'm not!' She glared at him and his face in front of her blurred as her eyes filled with tears.

'Then why the sudden attack of guilt?' He tugged her towards the bed and threw her down on it unceremoniously. 'If you're not ashamed, if there's no attack of guilt, then prove it. Touch me.'

Natalie looked away miserably. 'I can't.'

'Dammit, Natalie,' he muttered, and he sounded frustrated and uncertain. 'It's just sex.'

'That's exactly it,' she responded, 'just sex. But I'm not built like that.'

'No,' he said slowly, 'you're not, are you? It's commitment or nothing, isn't it?'

She shrugged. 'Is that so bad?'

'Why deny yourself pleasure simply because you want marriage at the end of it?' He knelt down by the bed and she could feel the urgency seeping out of him. 'Last night was wonderful. We could continue to enjoy each other; why spoil all that because you want to attach strings?'

'It's just the way I am,' Natalie said in a small voice. 'I knew you wouldn't understand. I know it's a dent to your pride . . .'

Kane gave a short, ironic laugh. 'My pride? Believe me, I think my pride will recover.'

'Yes,' she muttered, 'there will be enough women available to help you along the way, I'm sure.'

She edged across to the opposite side of the bed and they stared at each other like wary adversaries.

'What do you think I'm going to do?' Kane asked tersely, his mouth twisting. 'Rape you?'

After persuasion, Natalie thought, comes anger. Whatever he said, his pride would have been wounded by her refusal to have a short-lived affair with him.

'I think it's best if you left,' she said, ignoring his gibe. 'Talking about this isn't going to change my mind.'

He continued to stare at her for one long moment, then he picked up his various bits of clothing, sticking them on with jerky movements, not looking at her at all until he was standing by the bedroom door.

'You don't know what you're doing,' he said, his face clenched in angry lines.

'Right now,' Natalie replied with a great deal more bravado than she was feeling, 'I know exactly what I'm doing.' He had slipped on his clothes, a ridiculous outfit at five-thirty in the morning, and she felt a pang of pain so intense that she could scarcely breathe.

Was he right? Should she indulge her own physical desire for him to the detriment of everything else?

I've already done too much, she thought with bitterness. I've already let him see just what he can do to me. That had been a mistake.

She watched in silence as he let himself out of her bedroom, shutting the door behind him without a backward glance, then she got up from the bed and began straightening the room. With any luck she might just be able to straighten it all so much that she eradicated his presence completely. When she had done that, she sat on the bed and remained there, hearing all the little noises of the world outside coming to life.

She moved in a daze for the rest of the morning, shopping for food for the weekend, going to the gym where she rigourously worked out for over an hour, and for the first time ever didn't feel in the slightest bit better for it. She had to keep reminding herself that she had had no alternative but to ask him to leave, that her own stupidity had landed her in the mess, and it was just a good thing that some scrap of dignity and wisdom had given her the strength to salvage at least some of herself out of the disaster.

Several times the telephone rang, and each time she eyed it warily, half hoping it was Kane, but knowing realistically that it wouldn't be, and in no mood to talk to anyone at all. So she allowed it to ring.

By Sunday evening, she felt as though she had spent fifty years in solitary confinement. She was consoling herself with a cup of coffee, wondering whether a glass of wine might not be more appropriate and then remembering that there was none, when the doorbell went.

She jumped and stared at the door apprehensively. It couldn't be Kane, could it? It certainly wouldn't be Eric. He had told her that he would be visiting his parents in Shropshire on Sunday and Monday.

There was another demanding shrill from the doorbell and Natalie stood up. Why was she so scared? It was probably someone totally innocuous, maybe the Avon lady. She could handle an Avon lady without too many problems.

She pulled open the door and her face dropped. Not Kane, as she had dreaded, but not the Avon lady either. Anna. And, from the expression on her face, not in mood for light-hearted bantering either.

'Yes?' Natalie positioned herself in the middle of the doorway. 'What do you want?'

'To talk to you, of course. Why else do you imagine I would come here?' She glanced around her as though to imply that she would never normally venture into such an unsavoury neighbourhood. 'Can I come in?'

Natalie racked her brains for a suitable excuse for saying no, but couldn't think of any, and finally stood aside, watching Anna walk into her flat with a sinking feeling.

'Would you like some coffee?' Natalie forced a polite smile to her lips and was relieved when Anna shook her head impatiently.

'I don't intend to stay very long.'

Oh, good, Natalie thought, the shorter the better. She sat on the sofa at opposite ends to Anna and observed the other woman. Dressed to kill and looking quite out of place. Had she been somewhere first or did some people really hang around in silk tops and matching silk culottes? And all that make-up, Natalie thought cattily, must weigh a ton. Not to mention the hair piled on top of the head.

She smiled and felt a little better. 'So what can I do for you?'

'You can tell me why Kane has suddenly dropped me.'

There was a silence and Natalie hoped that she was managing to maintain a poker-still face, but she had her doubts. Her cheeks were burning furiously.

'He's dropped you?' she asked. 'I'm so sorry.'

Anna's full lips thinned. 'I doubt that. You never did care for me, did you? I was right about you, wasn't I? You wanted Kane for yourself and you intended to get him. I saw the way the two of you were on the weekend; I saw the way you were leading him on with those coy little looks, never mind your boyfriend in the background.'

'I wasn't leading anyone on!' Natalie protested furiously. Coy looks? For heaven's sake, she thought, that silly woman makes me sound like a Barbie doll.

'What did your boyfriend have to say about all of that?'

'Eric and I understand each other.' That, she knew, sounded awful, but if she denied a relationship with him, then Anna would have yet more cause for suspicion.

'That's awful. He seemed such a nice chap. How could you?'

'Excuse me?' Natalie looked at the other woman incredulously. 'In case it's escaped you, you happen to be

in my flat, sitting on my sofa. I don't have to listen to you preaching on my morality. So if you don't mind...'
She stood up, wondering why she hadn't done this sooner.

Anna stood up as well and her eyes were hard like diamonds. 'You stole my man,' she said with bitter spite in her voice. 'I know you did. Something happened between the two of you. He was mine and you took him from me. Well, I once warned you that revenge could be sweet. Now you'll find that out for yourself.'

She walked quickly towards the front door, her stiletto heels leaving little indentations on the carpet which Natalie found herself staring at in fascination, only pulling herself back to the other woman when the front door was open and the cool evening air brought the reality of the situation back to her.

'You don't frighten me,' Natalie said, meeting Anna's cold green gaze unflinchingly. 'You may think it acceptable to barge your way into my flat and threaten me with all sorts of vague things, but you're way off target if you think that I'm quaking in my shoes.'

'Oh, I don't care whether you're quaking in your shoes or not. All I intend to do is to teach you a lesson.' The hard, experienced mask slipped a little to reveal the spoilt little girl who had been thwarted, and Natalie realised with a sense of shock that Anna could only have been in her early-to-mid-twenties.

'Don't you think that's a little childish? If I can't persuade you that Kane Marshall means nothing to me, then don't you think that no man is worth this sort of reaction?'

'Don't patronise me!'

'I'm not.' Natalie sighed. 'If he's really broken off with you, then why don't you let it rest? He's surely not worth your regret.' Her voice had become thick with bitterness.

'Please don't act as though you know everything! You don't know the first thing about the relationship we had. I wanted him and I could have had him, I know it, but you came along with your new hairstyle and your new body and he saw you as a novelty. Well, I'll make sure that you pay for that! You'll know what it's like to have your man stolen from under your nose!'

There didn't seem a great deal left to say between them. Natalie felt sorry for the other woman. So much resentment in someone so young.

Kane Marshall, she thought, shutting the door against the cold, you have a lot to answer for. Playing games with other people's emotions, secure in the knowledge that his lack of commitment makes him invulnerable. It made her angry just thinking about it. Then she wondered what precisely Anna had meant by what she had threatened. Quite likely that passionate reaction would fizzle out by the time she turned the corner.

She went to bed early and lay awake in the dark bedroom, her eyes open, her mind whirring with everything that had happened over the past few weeks. Wouldn't it be nice, she thought, to be able to slide back into the past? But then the past had always been a fool's paradise.

She finally fell into a fitful sleep filled with disturbing nightmares, images that had her waking up in a sweat, praying for the steadying light of day to come.

Kane was not yet in when she arrived at work the following morning, which should have made things easier, but somehow didn't. It just seemed as though the inevitable was being delayed. She took off her summer jacket, and typed her letter quickly on the word processor, then she stuck it in a white envelope and placed it on Kane's desk. After that she tried to busy herself around the office, scrupulously tidying away odd bits of filing, catching up on letters that had been awaiting replies for the past couple of days.

She knew that Kane was coming almost before the office door opened. She didn't know whether it was some sort of telepathy born out of working so closely with him for so long, or whether his energy simply radiated out, announcing his presence before he had physically entered a room.

Whatever, she felt her nerves begin to jump and her whole body had tensed. He swept into the room like a hurricane, barely nodding in her direction, slamming his office door behind him, and Natalie's body went limp like rag.

What a pleasant way to start a Monday morning, she thought; what a lovely experience it's been working for you. She waited by her desk, knowing that sooner or later he would read her letter and confront her and wishing that she had given in to the cowardly urge to leave a message with one of the other secretaries.

He opened the door so silently that she barely heard it.

'What the hell is this?' he asked from behind her.

Natalie swivelled around. He was leaning against the door-frame, one hand in his trouser pocket, the other holding up her letter between two fingers, as though it were something deeply unhygienic. She cleared her throat and said in a toneless voice, 'It's my letter of resignation.'

'In my office. Now!' He swung around and Natalie reluctantly followed him into the room, not shutting the door behind her, subconsciously keeping her escape route open.

'I find this unacceptable,' he said shortly. He had sat down at his desk while she had remained standing, but somehow her position of superiority didn't fill her with confidence at all.

'I'm sorry.'

'Good. In that case, you can have it back and rip it into a thousand pieces. It belongs in the bin.'

'I can't do that,' Natalie said in a low voice and his eyebrows met in a threatening frown that sent a quiver of alarm down her spine.

'There's no such word as can't,' he informed her, and she didn't reply. She didn't want to argue, she didn't want to feel the power of his tongue, but on the other hand she had made up her mind to leave and there was nothing he could say or do that would convince her to stay.

It hadn't been an easy decision. She had worked for him for so long, had become so accustomed to postponing any decision to leave for another day, that finally doing the deed, resigning at last, had broken her heart. It was the dreadful finality of it. No more stolen glances, no more of that vibrancy which she felt whenever she was in his presence. It had to be done, but still hurt like hell. No amount of reasoning could lessen that. Her only hope was that he would never know how much.

'Well?' he barked angrily. 'Don't just stand there gaping, woman!'

'I've done all the filing,' Natalie informed him quietly, while inside everything continued to crumble, 'I've also answered that backlog of queries. Everything's in order for my replacement to take over.'

'You can't leave! You've just been promoted!'

'I realise that, and I'm sorry.' Her voice was a whisper. Beyond the sheer agony of knowing that she was creating her own empty vacuum by leaving, she doubted that she would be able to find another job that was either as satisfying or as well paid as the one she was leaving behind. And there would certainly never be another boss like Kane Marshall. She loved his ranting and raving, his thunderous bad tempers, his charm, his sense of fair play.

She swallowed hard. It was no good thinking about what she would miss. Kane Marshall had already absorbed far too much of her life. It would do her well to escape his stranglehold.

He was no longer staring at her. He had picked up his fountain pen and was fiddling with it. 'If you want an apology for what happened the other night, then you have it.'

'I didn't ask for an apology.' Natalie didn't want to discuss this; she would much rather have pretended that it had never happened. 'Besides, I'm not going to pretend that I was an innocent party. It takes two.'

'We can put it behind us. A mistake. They happen.' He glared at her and she shook her head.

'I...'

'I won't be chasing you around the desk, if that's what you're so damned afraid of,' he snapped. 'That's what's bothering you, isn't it? You think that we won't be able to resume our working relationship, but we will. Trust me.'

Trust you? The thought made her want to laugh out loud, or scream, or cry or *something*.

'It's not that...'

'Then what the hell is it?'

He looked at her directly and she couldn't think of what reply to give him. Certainly not the truth—that she was desperately in love with him, that every day in his company would be an arrow through her heart, that sleeping with him had been the biggest mistake in her life because it had taken away all her illusions. It had shown her that at the end of the day, even when the impossible had happened and he had wanted her, he had only wanted her for a while, to fill a passing need until someone else came along. How could she explain any of that to him?

'I've been here a long time,' Natalie began shakily, 'five years. I've gained a lot of experience and now I just feel that it's time to move on.'

It was flattering that he wanted her to stay, he made no attempt to hide it, but it hurt that it was only on a working level that she would ever be indispensable to him. Then she laughed bitterly to herself. Good grief, had she ever expected otherwise? There was a place for girlish dreams and this was not it.

'Where will you go?' His voice was cold, and she realised that he had accepted the inevitable. He might not like it because her departure would interfere badly with the orderly workings of his office, but he accepted it and with that acceptance came cold indifference. Did he really give a damn where she went?

Natalie shrugged. 'I have no idea.'

He stood up and went across to the window, looking down at the busy street below. 'I won't expect you to work out your notice.'

'Thank you.'

There was an awkward silence, then Natalie stood up. 'If you don't mind,' she began, and he nodded curtly, not bothering to turn to face her.

'You must drop by and let us all know how you get on in your new job,' he said politely.

What a relief that he wasn't looking at her, she thought, and couldn't see how close to bursting into tears she was.

'I will.'

She walked out of the room quickly, and then out of the office, stopping on her way down to say goodbye to all of the people she had come to know over the years. Heaven only knew what they were thinking. No doubt there would be the usual speculative gossip as soon as she left the building.

It was only when she was outside that it hit her. The void of knowing that she would never see Kane Marshall again. It was almost as if the threads that had been holding her life together had suddenly been taken away, and had left her floundering and unsure. What was she going to do next? Oh, she would find a job, but the vastness of the space which Kane's absence from her life created would be infinitely more difficult to fill.

She spent the afternoon on the telephone and realised very quickly that no job was going to match her salary. The following day she took herself down to all of the agencies and busied herself with the time-consuming business of filling in forms.

By the end of the week, she had been to several interviews, but nothing compared to working with Kane. It was an effort to keep reminding herself that she would just have to accept that that part of her life was gone forever.

Eric seemed bewildered by her decision.

'But I thought that you enjoyed it,' he said, perplexed. 'I mean, up to a fortnight ago you were putting yourself out to entertain his clients!'

'Exactly.'

'Exactly?'

'I woke up one morning and decided that a change was as good as a rest.'

'So now you're out of work.'

'Something like that,' Natalie admitted. She must have sounded more depressed than she wanted to because later that evening she found herself in a restaurant with him, and his sympathy was so tangible that she found herself cheering up quite a bit.

Over their second bottle of wine, she was laughing much more than she would have thought possible in her frame of mind, and by the third bottle Eric had succeeded in coming up with a magnificent idea.

'What,' he said loudly, 'about going to work for one of your clients? Our people——' was that a hiccup? '—do it all the time. Leave the profession and work for a client.' He gesticulated broadly. 'All the time.'

Natalie had never thought of that, but why not? On the Monday, she phoned one of her clients who had jokingly promised her a job if she should ever need one, and by Tuesday she was employed. She could have kissed Eric. Instead, she telephoned him and invited out to a meal.

'Tonight,' she said, 'you name the place. After all, it was your idea.'

His voice was decidedly vague when he replied. 'Tonight's a bit tricky, Natalie. What about tomorrow?'

'I don't know, Eric,' she said, a bit deflated. 'I'm not sure what time I'll be back.' They left it for some other, unspecified day, and Natalie promptly put it to the back of her mind.

Somehow, she thought a few days later, working for Tony Harding made her feel as though she had not lost touch completely with Kane. They were a small outfit, but an up-and-coming one, and her job involved doing quite a bit of nearly everything, from taking calls to dealing with customers. The money was meagre compared to what she had been getting at her old job, and the excitement of working for a leading company was absent, but in its place was the comfort of working for someone whom she had spoken to on the phone countless times, who showed her the ropes, and who left her to get on with it.

And, she had to admit, it was cheap on clothes. Because the office site was something along the lines of a warehouse, jeans were the order of the day. Her suits remained hanging in her wardrobe, reminders of other times. She could associate each and every one with Kane, some occasion, some incident. In the end she removed them to the wardrobe in the spare room simply so that they would no longer confront her on a daily basis.

She was updating their system of logging invoices, one of the projects which she had set herself from early on because the disorder had been getting on her nerves, when some sixth sense made her look up to find a pair of brilliant green eyes staring at her laconically from the doorway. Kane Marshall, and, next to him, Tony.

Natalie stared at him. She felt as though it had literally been years since she had laid eyes on him, even though it had only been a matter of a couple of weeks or so. Every fibre in her body awakened in his sudden presence, then she collected herself together with a little shake and stood up.

Tony bustled into the room, overweight, red-faced and enthusiastic. Kane followed him, looking around the building, then fixing his gaze on her until Natalie felt colour creeping up her skin.

How could she have pretended to herself that her new job had done anything to diminish the effect he had on her? That she would ever be able to conveniently forget him?

'A nice little job for you, Natalie,' Tony said with a beaming smile and Natalie dragged her eyes away from Kane. 'Lunch with your ex-boss. I'm hoping you'll be able to use your privileged position to talk him into some reduced rates for me.' Kane was looking at her with an ironic expression on his face, as though daring her to come up with some excuse for refusing the offer.

'What about those letters you wanted me to type?' she ventured weakly and Tony laughed.

'They'll wait. This is more important.' He glanced at the two of them and she could see that he was trying to figure out why she was so unenthusiastic about the idea. Most people would have jumped at the idea of an all-expenses-paid lunch, and especially if it was with someone they had known for five years.

But Tony would never put two and two together. His mind was too involved with his growing business. The personal details of other people's lives around him passed him by.

'I'll just get my jacket,' Natalie mumbled, the hairs on the back of her neck tingling as she felt Kane's eyes on her.

What, she wanted to know, was he doing here anyway? Hadn't he done enough to her already? She had the depressing, desperate feeling that she had been catapulted right back to square one.

She joined Kane in Reception where he was discussing one of Tony's projects and when she walked in they both looked up. She smiled at Tony, then turned to Kane and her face was perfectly controlled.

'Are you ready?'

'Whenever you are,' Kane murmured, holding the door open for her to walk past him, which she did. Very quickly.

She stepped into his car, a sleek burgundy Jaguar, her body tensing as he slid into the seat alongside her. Then he turned to face her, his hands on the steering-wheel.

'I've missed you, Natalie,' he said huskily.

Natalie's breathing quickened. 'I take it my replacement hasn't quite got used to the ropes as yet?'

There was a short silence, then he said abruptly, 'She's hopeless. A temp. One of several who have come and gone.' He started up the engine and the car roared into life. 'I don't suppose you would reconsider coming back?'

'No.'

'I didn't think so. Harding treating you that well, eh?'

I can cope with him, she wanted to say, which is something to be grateful for.

'I'm very busy. How did you find out where I worked anyway?' she asked, still not daring to look at him because to do so would be to confront the hopeless fact that she was still head over heels in love with him, that he could still thrill her merely by being there. 'Or was it sheer coincidence your being here?'

'He telephoned me for a reference on you,' Kane told her, and she nodded in comprehension. That possibility had never even crossed her mind. If it had, she might have not been quite so eager to take a job so close to home.

'Why did you come?' she asked quietly. 'I know you. You only ever visit massive clients. You delegate the smaller ones.'

He glanced across at her. 'I came because I still want you, Natalie Robins,' he told her in a cool voice. 'No woman runs out on me. Don't you know there's nothing more challenging to someone like me than the inaccessible? I took you once. I intend to do it again.'

CHAPTER EIGHT

NATALIE wanted desperately to laugh this off as a joke, but there was something deadly serious in that silky voice. Panic snaked through her, making her dizzy.

'You can't be serious,' she said shakily, licking her lips to moisten them. She stared straight ahead of her, not wanting to face him because she was scared of what she might see there. His anger, his arrogance, his cynicism—those were things that she could cope with. His pursuit was not. That was dangerous because it exposed her vulnerability to him, and she wasn't going to fall into that trap a second time.

'Why not?' he answered coolly, his hand resting lightly on the gear shaft.

Natalie eyed it in trepidation and edged away. If the car were at a standstill right now, she had no doubt that she would have flung open the door and run as fast as her legs could take her. Her heart was beating so quickly that she had the giddy sensation that any minute she would choke to death. She forced the panic back. That, she knew, was not going to help her. What she needed to fight his devastating relentlessness was calm.

She breathed deeply and tried very hard to summon up a feeling of calm. Pretend, she told herself, that he isn't Kane Marshall. Pretend that he's simply an ordinary, paunchy, balding businessman sitting there, making a pest of himself. She closed her eyes and filled her mind with the image, immediately feeling more in control.

She gave a little laugh. 'Why not?' she repeated with a hint of amusement in her voice. 'I can think of several thousand reasons, but the main one is I don't want it.'

'No?' He shot her a sideways glance and some of that exquisite control slipped slightly. 'We could always put that to the test.'

'No, we could not!' Natalie replied sharply. 'This isn't some kind of game. If you feel the urge to chase a woman, then do me a favour and find another one to chase. I have a new job and,' she continued with sudden inspiration, 'I'm trying to build a relationship with Eric.'

The car pulled over to the kerb and Natalie glanced at him uneasily. She hoped that he wasn't about to try anything, because she knew that a single touch from him would be enough to shatter her will-power to shreds. She clutched the door-handle and he said with lazy amusement, 'Relax. I'm not about to jump on you in this public place.'

'I never said you were,' Natalie answered quickly.

'You didn't have to. You looked like a scared rabbit about to dash into the nearest hole. Are you?'

'Am I what?'

'Scared of me? Afraid of what might happen to you if I lay a finger on you?'

Everything about him, his voice, the way he was sitting there, lightly resting against the door, was controlled and unhurried. He was in absolutely no rush whatsoever, and the fact that she had told him, quite firmly, that she had no intention of sleeping with him didn't appear to bother him in the slightest. In fact, Natalie thought angrily, he seemed to be relishing the situation.

'Are we going to have some lunch?' she asked coolly. 'Because if we aren't I have a million things to do back at the office.'

Kane laughed softly and she had the frightening feeling that he viewed her protestations as delaying tactics that would not possibly defer the inevitable.

'Lunch, by all means,' he drawled, letting himself out of the car and moving around to open her door for her. Natalie shot out, her arm burning where it brushed against his.

They dined at a pleasant Italian bistro without a hint of the suffocating intimacy which Natalie had expected, and Kane kept up amusing conversation on an array of subjects.

Very crafty, she thought, making sure that he doesn't frighten his prey away. Not that it was going to work. She responded politely, interested in what he had to say about what was going on at the Marshall Corporation, amused by his witty anecdotes and quite happy to chat to him about her new job.

When they were leaving the restaurant, he bent slightly towards her and said in a lazy undertone, 'I never answered your question, did I?'

Natalie pulled back, alarmed at the slow tingle of heat that had spread through her body by his proximity.

'What question?' she asked briskly, standing back to allow him to open the car door for her, and then slipping inside very quickly. Kane leisurely opened his door, but instead of starting up the engine he turned in his seat to look at her, his eyes doing a very careful appraisal of her flushed face.

'You wanted to know why I didn't occupy my time chasing other women.'

Natalie stared straight ahead of her while her heart did funny things in her chest. After the fairly relaxing, unthreatening light-hearted banter over lunch, the sudden casual intimacy in Kane's tone alarmed her, though she didn't want to give him the satisfaction of showing it.

'I'm not really that curious,' she said.

'I'm not chasing other women, because right now there's only one woman I'm interested in chasing.'

Right now, she thought bitterly. He certainly was an expert at introducing lack of permanence in his relationships, wasn't he? She looked at him coldly. 'It was a very pleasant lunch. Why do you have to spoil it?'

'Is that what I'm doing?' He reached out to stroke the side of her face with one finger and she pulled back. His eyes, smiling, flickered over her. He was playing a waiting game. Biding his time, content to let minor obstacles such as her objections be trampled by time and patience.

'I'm not interested.'

'No,' Kane agreed with a hint of laughter in his voice, 'just so long as it's only me you're not interested in.'

He started up the car, expertly manoeuvring it through the crowded streets back to Tony Harding's offices, which were in a far less plush, and consequently much cheaper, part of London.

'I'll be seeing you,' he said as the car stopped in front of the building, and Natalie shook her head vehemently.

'I'm busy.'

'So am I,' Kane said, as though he was agreeing with her over some innocuous statement like, Isn't it hot today?

She glared at him helplessly. 'Why me?' she asked on a high whisper. 'You never used to look at me twice.'

'What makes you say that?' he asked with interest.

Natalie frowned, disconcerted and puzzled by his response. 'We had a good working relationship,' she said. 'I would have known if you had been interested in me in that way. I know there was that stupid Christmas party, but that doesn't count.' She laughed shortly. 'Don't forget I had an awful lot of experience of seeing you in action with other women. I would have recognised one of those deliberately charming looks from a mile away.'

'I don't think I care for that description,' Kane informed her, his voice half-offended, half-amused.

It was one-thirty and groups of people were trooping back into the building, some of them idly glancing at the parked Jaguar. The four-storeyed structure housed several companies, though Natalie was beginning to recognise some of the faces of people she saw intermittently in the lift, even though they did not work with her.

It was a warm day and there was a general air of reluctance about their slow-paced return to work. Natalie herself was reluctant to go back inside the hot building. There was no air-conditioning, which meant the small windows had to be pushed open to their maximum, not that that encouraged a great deal of ventilation.

She indulged in a wild, brief fantasy of driving somewhere with Kane. To a secluded beach somewhere perhaps. Making love on the sand. The image was so vivid that she felt her cheeks burn and immediately opened her car door.

'It's true,' Natalie said quietly, dragging her thoughts back to the present. 'You only noticed me after I lost weight and found a boyfriend.'

'You were never overweight.'

'Ha!' Natalie laughed incredulously. 'Do you really expect me to believe that?'

'No,' Kane said, 'but it's the truth nevertheless. You lost weight and *you* changed—you began to notice men's reactions to you instead of simply assuming that they weren't interested.'

'That's not true,' Natalie denied automatically; but was he right? Confusion swept over her and her hand was trembling when she pushed the car door open.

'I have to go,' she muttered, and he caught her by her wrist, wrenching her slightly so that she had to twist around to look at him.

'I'm going to see you again, Natalie. You can't run away from me, so don't even bother to try. And I mean what I say—you're mine, reserved for me and no one else.'

'Don't tell me what to do!'

'I want you.'

Natalie looked at him furiously. 'I have to go,' she repeated, and he released her. With a swift movement, she let herself out of the car, hurrying up towards the building, resisting the temptation to look around and see whether he was still sitting there in his car, looking at her.

Her head was hurting by the time she made it back to her office. Should she be flattered at his determination, she wondered, or insulted? He assumed, despite everything she had said to him, that he would sooner or later achieve his objective in seducing her, but was it really so surprising? She doubted he had ever failed with a woman. He had that fatally potent combination of good looks, intelligence and charm which most women would find impossible to resist.

Tony grinned at her absent-mindedly when she swept into the office and asked her how lunch went.

'Fine,' Natalie replied vaguely.

'Managed to cut any deals for me?' he joked, and Natalie thought, If only you knew. The subject hadn't even arisen.

She seemed to spend the next week looking over her shoulder, wondering whether he was going to spring any surprise visits on her, and quite prepared to hide under her bed if he did.

But there was no sign of him. Maybe, she thought, he had found himself another woman. The thought was so sickening that she shoved it to the back of her mind, then immediately told herself off for being a fool. She should be hoping that he did find someone else, because that would at least deflect him away from her and give her the peace of mind she wanted to crave.

It didn't help that just when she needed the calm company of Eric he was becoming elusive. Appointments seemed to be springing up all over the place for him until she teased light-heartedly, 'You're avoiding me, aren't you?'

'No, of course not!' Eric exclaimed, but was there the tiniest element of sheepishness behind his denial?

Later, when they met for a meal in one of the wine bars in the West End, he confessed, red-faced, that he had been dating another woman.

Natalie laughed, delighted. 'Who?'

'Another totally unsuitable woman,' he admitted, sipping from his glass of wine and shaking his head wistfully.

Natalie nodded sympathetically. Didn't she know first hand what he was going through? Except she was desperately trying to avoid her totally unsuitable man. Presumably Eric still had some control over his life and his emotions and had not lost both the way she stupidly had.

She was so engrossed with her problems, that frantic desire to never clap eyes on Kane Marshall ever again mixed with a shameful yearning for everything he could give her, her job, that she assumed that nothing further could complicate her life. There was a limit to how cruel fate could be, wasn't there?

At first, she pretended to herself that it just couldn't be, that those bouts of nausea which seemed to be getting more frequent were simply the outcome of an upset stomach. Or stress. Probably the two, she decided.

On the fourth day she convinced herself that it had been a total waste of money purchasing a home pregnancy kit. On the sixth day, she decided that she might as well get value for her wasted money by at least using the damn thing. Complete waste of time, she told herself, as she sat in the lounge and waited for the kit to back her up.

The positive result was such a shock that Natalie stared at it for fifteen minutes in horrified silence, overcome by the urge to faint.

It couldn't be true. She tried to think clearly, but it was difficult. She wanted to collapse. She closed her eyes and opened them again very slowly, thinking that perhaps she had imagined the whole thing. But she had not.

In the end she phoned her sister, but instead of explaining the situation she chatted about everything else, her voice bright and cheerful, and hung up feeling even more isolated and frightened than ever.

What was she going to do? Darkness gathered around her and she remained sitting in the lounge, not bothering to switch on the lights. Nothing that had ever happened in her life before could have prepared her for this. The shock, the frightening reality of it, deadened her until her brain became sluggish and could only revolve around and around on the same lines. A baby. In her. Kane's baby—and what the hell was she going to do?

She didn't hear the knocking on the door, wasn't aware of the dark figure pushing it open then moving quickly towards her. At least, she wasn't aware of the dark figure until he was kneeling in front of her, his face barely discernible in the dark. Then she sprang up, her face white.

'What are you doing here?' she asked in a high, uneven voice.

Kane stood up, his eyes urgent and penetrating.

'I knocked but there was no answer so I pushed the door and it was open. What the hell is going on here? Why are you sitting here in darkness?'

Natalie stared at him mutely. Seeing Kane here, like this, had thrown her into a state of shock and she felt as though she would choke if she tried talking.

'Answer me!' He gripped her by her elbows and shook her slightly, sending her hair flying around her face.

It galvanised her frozen mind back into action and she wrenched herself free.

'I told you I didn't want to see you,' she said quickly and desperately. 'I told you. So get out.' Her voice was rising with each syllable and Kane was staring at her with a bemused frown. He knew that something was very wrong, but he couldn't figure out what. Natalie laughed out loud and the laughter sounded shrill and uncontrolled even in her own ears.

'What's happened?' he demanded, striding over to the light-switch and turning on the lights.

Natalie put her hands to her face. Anyone would think that he was concerned about her. He deserved an Oscar for the performance.

'Nothing,' she said fighting to keep her voice steady and so not arouse his suspicions even further. 'I had a bit of a headache, that's all.' She rubbed her temples. Her head really did hurt as well. It hurt with all the pain and confusion she was feeling inside. They said that your emotions could make you physically ill.

Kane moved over to the sofa and sat beside her, his body depressing the cushions and making her dip slightly towards him. From this close, his clean masculine scent filled her head like incense, and it was an effort to remember that small fact of her pregnancy, lying there like a time bomb waiting to explode.

All of a sudden, her mind became very lucid. Whereas before she had been swept up in a whirlpool of sickening panic, now, ironically with him sitting right there by her, she thought quickly and clearly.

He must not find out. That seemed to be the most important thing. She had no intention of terminating the pregnancy. On the other hand, she was not going to confront him with it either. She half suspected that he would feel obliged to do the honourable thing and get her up to the altar, and Natalie could think of nothing worse than a marriage conceived for the wrong reasons.

It was a tremendous struggle, though, not to succumb to that alluring desire to crack up, to rant and rave and share her terrible anguish with the man who had created it, because ironically he would have been the one person who would have understood. But there was no way that she could afford to do that.

No, she had to be sensible. Her impassioned rejection of him had merely served to stoke his interest. She would have to try another tack altogether. Indifference. That, if nothing else, would be guaranteed to kill any curiosity he might have about her potential as a short-term affair.

'Can I get you a cup of coffee?' she asked, venturing a smile.

Kane's frown deepened. He was not stupid. He knew that there was something suspicious about her sudden mood-switch, but he could not work out what. He shook his head and continued to look at her.

'What about something cold?' she pressed. 'I don't tend to have a great deal of alcohol in the house, but——'

'How come the sudden hostess act?' he interrupted drily. He sat back in the sofa and folded his arms. 'Don't tell me that your headache has brought on a change of temperament.'

'I'm always a good hostess,' Natalie informed him, twisting her fingers nervously together, and immediately pulling herself up short when he noticed the unconscious motion.

'Let me get you something.' He stood up and flexed his arms, and she followed the movement with hungry absorption. 'You don't exactly look very good. You're as white as a sheet. I had no idea you were prone to such bad headaches. You never had them when you were working for me.' He paused and then said mockingly, 'Maybe working for Tony Harding doesn't agree with you.'

Wouldn't you like me to agree to that one? Natalie thought bitterly. Then you could use all that charm to try and persuade me that working for you would take care of all my headaches. And you'd have all the time in the world to plan and execute your seduction.

The thought was so nightmarish that she actually shuddered. She had no idea how pregnant she was, but sooner or later she would begin to show, and when that time arrived she would have to make sure that she was as far as possible away from Kane Marshall, even if it meant buying herself a one-way ticket to Timbuktu.

'It's been a bit muggy today,' she offered by way of feeble explanation. 'That's probably it.'

'Now, what can I get you?'

Natalie looked up at him and sighed. He wasn't about to leave and there was no point in forcing the issue. That would just convince him that something really was wrong, and once he began thinking along those lines it would only be a matter of time before he arrived at the correct explanation. He was damned clever and very shrewd with it.

'There's some orange juice in the fridge,' she said, defeated, and he vanished towards the kitchen.

Natalie lay back and stared at the ceiling. Why couldn't her life have been straightforward? she asked herself. Why did she have to go and fall in love with Kane Marshall, and then, to top it off, find herself pregnant by him? It was all her fault, of course, but pointing the finger of blame wasn't going to change anything.

When he returned to the lounge he was carrying a plate of scrambled eggs on toast, as well as the glass of juice, both of which he deposited on the coffee-table in front of her. The gesture brought a lump to Natalie's throat. She knew that he could be thoughtful, she had seen evidence of it in the past, but right now that particular trait didn't help matters at all.

'Thank you,' she murmured huskily. 'You needn't have gone to all this bother.'

He sat next to her and grinned. 'Believe me, scrambled eggs on toast don't rate as cordon-bleu cooking.'

Natalie looked across at him and their eyes tangled.

'You know what I mean,' she said, addled. It tasted good too, she thought, looking away and digging into the plateful of food. She was hungrier than she had thought. Starving, in fact. There was something terribly relaxing about his presence just now. Unthreatening and comfortable. She must be losing her mind, she decided. All the same, it was nice to have someone with her. And not just someone, the father of her baby. The enormity of the thought brought a flush of colour to her cheeks.

'I had no idea you were this domestic,' she said in a rush, to hide the sudden flare of panic. 'Egg on toast, orange juice.' She laughed nervously. 'I know it's not *haute cuisine*, but I still never associated cooking with you.'

There was a little silence, then Kane said with a mixture of levity and seriousness, 'Nor did I.'

She scraped the plate clean and gave a little sigh. Oh, wouldn't it be nice to pretend that this fantasy could last forever? To be able to pretend that she could actually climb out of this awful whirlpool into which she had been sucked?

'Headache feeling any better?' he asked and she nodded, her eyes half closed. 'Your colour's returned,' he informed her.

'Being nice to me isn't going to get me into bed with you,' Natalie said, her voice sharp and defensive, and Kane threw her an impatient frown.

'Are you usually so suspicious?'

'Only with you.' She looked at him levelly, knowing that she would have to make him understand, somehow, that she was not available, and that persistence was not going to pay off eventually, which was the illusion he appeared to be harbouring.

'Thank you for making me feel so special. Can't you control that tendency of yours for honesty just a little bit?' He strolled across to the window and stared outside, his back to her.

Go away, she wanted to scream. Leave me alone with my problems! I'm having your baby and I'm scared to death and your being here just makes everything worse!

'It isn't going to work,' she said bluntly, ignoring his gibe.

'You're attracted to me,' he rasped, turning around to look at her, semi-perched on the window-ledge.

'It was a mistake,' Natalie pleaded. 'I know I was attracted to you, but I'm not like that. I don't want to have an affair with you.'

'Well, then marry me,' he said carelessly.

Natalie looked at him, stunned. 'What?'

'Marry me.' He shrugged.

'You don't believe in marriage. You told me.' She unconsciously rested the flat of her hand on her stomach and momentarily lost herself in the fantasy of being Kane Marshall's wife.

He lowered his eyes so that she couldn't read the expression on his face. 'Perhaps it's inescapable.' His head snapped up and he glared at her. 'Aren't you flattered that I'm willing to take that step just to get you into my bed?'

'And aren't you relieved when I tell you that I would never even consider it?'

'Why not?' he asked aggressively, walking towards her. 'You once gave me a great long lecture on the importance of marriage and commitment. So I'm offering it to you. It's the most any woman's ever got out of me.'

Things were so black and white with him, Natalie thought. Did he really imagine for a moment that she would marry him simply to satiate his lust? And what about when he got bored with her? Divorce? Or maybe he would just tuck her away in his country house and pick up the threads of his other women in London.

And what about the baby? He might let her go, but he would never let his child go. That was something she knew instinctively. And then, if she did marry him, would he jump to the conclusion that she had got herself pregnant on purpose and forced him into a back-handed marriage by holding out on sexual favours?

It was a sickening thought and she had no intention of letting it even cross his mind.

'Thank you for the proposal of marriage,' she said stiffly, 'but I'm afraid I can't oblige.'

'For God's sake, woman, what the hell else do you want?' he thundered furiously. Dented pride, she thought, what rage it inspired.

'I don't want anything from you. Can't you understand that?'

'No.' He gave her an angry, bewildered look.

Natalie said with a catch in her voice, 'When I was young, and I imagined being proposed to, I always thought that there would be a touch of romance about it.' She was thinking her thoughts out loud rather then levelling a criticism, but he immediately rushed to his defence.

'Are you saying that you want more romance? I'll give you flowers,' he muttered darkly. 'You just never struck me as the sentimental sort.'

'I'm sorry. It's no good.'

'Fine.' He stood up and that hurt pride had transformed itself into coldness. 'I don't intend to beg.'

'I didn't think that I had asked you to.' If only she could say something trite, like, Couldn't we please still remain friends? But she knew that that would not have been acceptable to him, and if it had been it would be a disaster anyway. So she hung her head and stared in fascination at her fingers.

He walked across to the door and paused with his hand on the doorknob.

'I hope that poor sucker knows what he's letting himself in for,' he snarled. 'Does he know that you intend to twist him round your little finger?'

That stung. He made her sound like a dragon.

'I don't intend to do any such thing,' she retaliated, her anger beginning to match his.

'Well, good luck. You'll damn well need it if you're going to settle down with that half-wit of an accountant.'

He left the flat, slamming the door shut behind him, and Natalie stared at it for several minutes before getting up and clearing away her plate and glass—reminders of a side to him that she did not want to recall.

She took the next morning off work to go and see her doctor, a boy who looked years younger than herself and did not seem in the slightest bit perturbed that she was unmarried.

'All seems fine,' he said, 'and I needn't tell you that you can continue working pretty much to the end.' He ran through the usual routine things, but his words had set her mind reeling off on a new tangent.

Work. Of course, she would have to leave before the pregnancy became noticeable. She could not have Tony revealing to Kane that she was pregnant. That would be a disaster. Why hadn't she thought of this before?

On the spur of the moment she decided to take the remainder of the week off and visit her sister. Selina lived in the country with her husband and children, and could be relied upon to make Natalie forget some of her troubles. She was placid and understanding.

Natalie relaxed there for four days, hugging her secret to herself, waiting for just the right moment to confide, and then departed without having said a word. Her sister

was not at all old-fashioned, but somehow Natalie
thought that she would be shocked. Pregnancy outside
marriage, and a relationship for that matter, would not
have shocked her, but the fact that her sister was the
one pregnant would have. And right now Natalie couldn't
deal with that sort of reaction.

She returned to London to find that Eric had been
calling her persistently at work.

'I need to see you,' he told her, when she finally found
the time and the energy to return his calls. They arranged to meet at one of the bistros which was close to
the Marshall Corporation and which Natalie had grown
fond of over the past few years. It was cosy without
being claustrophobic and the prices were affordable.
Quite a few of the secretaries frequented it because they
could enjoy a pleasant evening there without having to
take out a bank loan for the privilege.

Eric was waiting when she walked in. She had managed
to dash back to the flat to change before meeting him,
and was dressed in a very summery, cool apricot dress
which nipped in to the waist and then fell to just above
her knees. It was one of her most comfortable dresses,
and she had chosen it out of a perverse sense of irony.
After all, with that tailored waist, it would probably be
one of the first things she would have to put into cold
storage when her body started expanding.

Eric ordered her a glass of orange juice, only expressing polite surprise that she wasn't drinking, and then
proceeded to peer at her guiltily over the rim of his glass.

'I've got a confession to make,' he said, once they had
covered the preliminary chit-chat.

Natalie looked at him, surprised out of her intro-
spection. She had no idea what this was leading up to
and she was curious to find out. Eric looked extremely

red-faced and embarrassed and she wondered what on earth he had to confess. Some secret side to him that he felt she ought to know about? She hoped not. She couldn't handle any complications in someone else's life. Her own was too complicated as it was.

'What confession?' she asked warily.

'I know we've been seeing an awful lot of each other——' he cleared his throat and glanced at her '—and I hope you haven't—I know I'm just being a fool when I say this, but I do hope you haven't, that you don't...'

'I haven't,' Natalie reassured him, reading his mind, 'and I don't. There was never anything serious between us and that was one reason why being with you was so enjoyable.' She summoned up a smile, the first genuine one for what seemed like years, and he looked hugely relieved.

'It's just that I know that this might be a bit of surprise to you, but I'm going to be married.'

Natalie looked at him, astounded. 'You sly dog,' she said slowly. 'Married? Can I ask who the lucky girl is?'

Eric looked down and twiddled with the stem of his wine glass. 'You know her, actually.' He raised his eyes to her. 'Anna. Your boss's ex-girlfriend.'

Anna. Anna and her threats to show her what it felt like to have her man stolen. Was this her revenge? Stealing Eric? And had that revenge turned into something unexpected? Surely it had to be the latter. After all, marriage was a heavy price to pay to even a debt, and Natalie could not see the other woman paying it simply for that reason.

'You really are a sly one,' she said, keeping her thoughts to herself, then with a gesture of affection she leaned across the narrow table and threw her arms around his neck, kissing him soundly on the mouth—a totally sexless kiss that spelt fondness and nothing more.

And as she raised her eyes she met familiar green ones staring at her from across the room. Cool, assessing and not very friendly. And across the table from him a pair of blue eyes gazed with open lust at his face. Blue eyes that belonged to a long body, jet-black hair and the face of an unknown woman who looked like an angel.

Suddenly Natalie didn't feel quite so happy any more.

CHAPTER NINE

HER face was pink when she sat back down in her chair, but Eric merely assumed that it was because she was taken aback, surprised and thrilled at his revelation. And Natalie made no attempt to disillusion him. Nor did she inform him that her ex-boss—and Anna's ex-lover—was sitting behind him, a few tables away.

Besides, she had a feeling that it would have gone in one ear and out of the other. He was far too busy chattering away about his fiancée, expressing wonder at his luck in having had his proposal of marriage accepted.

'Of course, my parents are going to be a little disappointed,' he said with a grin. 'I think they wanted to see me happily settled with someone slightly less flamboyant, but you know love.'

Natalie laughed vaguely and her eyes slipped across the room to where Kane was now looking at the woman at his table, a warm smile curving his lips.

So much for my long-lasting impact on him, she thought. She tried her best to be philosophical; after all, wasn't this just precisely what she wanted? But it was difficult being philosophical when salt was being rubbed into an open wound.

When Eric excused himself to go to the men's room, it was almost a relief to have silence. She looked miserably down into her cup of coffee and swirled it between her fingers, watching the liquid form patterns in the cup. When was this piercing ache ever going to leave her? She glanced up at Kane and her whole body quivered with remembered longing. She had loved this man for years, had always known that it would lead nowhere. Surely that should make her feelings easier to control? Surely that should numb the bitter jealousy spreading through her at the thought of that unknown woman in bed with him?

Because there was very little doubt that that was where their evening was heading. All those coy looks in between provocative tossing of her black mane were not destined to a cup of cocoa in front of the television. Cups of cocoa weren't Kane Marshall's style at all, Natalie thought acidly, and from the looks of the woman in his company they weren't hers either.

'Of course, you'll come,' Eric was saying as he sat back down and beckoned the waiter across for the bill.

Natalie looked at him blankly.

'To the wedding,' he explained patiently, 'Next week Friday. A simple affair at a register office. I'll phone and give you all the details.'

She nodded absent-mindedly, and Eric looked satisfied. He paid the bill, his face still wreathed in smiles at the prospect of tying the knot, and they went directly back to her flat. Natalie kissed him on the cheek, then gave him a hug, and let herself into her empty home.

She felt dull and lifeless, and horribly weighed down with the knowledge of her pregnancy. It was usually a cause for celebration with most women, she thought sadly, yet here I am, hiding it as if it's something shameful.

The doorbell went and Natalie thought, Eric. She hoped he hadn't decided on the spur of the moment to invite himself in for a cup of coffee, or a nightcap. She felt exhausted from his perky banter. Right now she needed privacy in which to wallow in her self-pity.

Tomorrow she would start cultivating her usual optimism.

She swung open the door but it wasn't Eric standing on the doorstep. It was Kane. Behind him, she could see Eric's car vanishing to the end of the street. They must have crossed paths. She looked at him belligerently, blaming him for everything she was going through. What was he doing here? This was all his fault. She wished that she had never clapped eyes on him. Why couldn't he have been ugly? Why couldn't he have been married with ten kids and a devoted wife? She wouldn't have looked twice at him then. Most of all, why couldn't he have left her alone and not made love to her out of some twisted desire to satiate his curiosity?

She uncomfortably shoved to the back of her mind the thought that she had not exactly spurned his advances. Now she glared at him and was pushing the door shut when he shouldered his way in to stand inside the landing, his green eyes like chips of ice.

'You have no right to barge your way into this flat!' Natalie shot out. '*My* flat!' Already she felt close to tears. Maybe it was the hormones, or maybe it was anger. Whatever, she turned away abruptly and blinked away the awful desire to cry.

'I can't believe that you're still seeing that man,' Kane said tightly.

'You followed me here to tell me *that*?' She gave a laugh that bordered dangerously on the hysterical.

He gripped her by her arms, his black brows meeting in a furious frown. 'I spoke to him before I came in here,' he bit out, and Natalie looked at him warily.

Spoke to Eric? What about? Kane had never had anything very pleasant to say about him, so what could they possibly have to discuss?

'What about?' she asked tentatively, going limp in his clutch because it was futile putting up any kind of fight with him.

'What do you think?' he grated, shaking her slightly so that she winced in discomfort. 'What do you bloody think?' There was real burning rage in his eyes. What was going on here? Was she missing something? He had known of Eric's presence in her life for long enough. In fact, she had done her best to exaggerate the whole thing, and he had so far never reacted with such intense, cold fury to the knowledge.

Besides, as far as they were both concerned, whatever brief encounter they had shared was over and done with. It was imperative that she get on with her life, vanish out of his waters forever, and she wished that he would leave her alone.

Maybe, she thought desperately, he was obsessed with having her. Like a fisherman who became obsessed with catching the fish that got away. Was that it? What was she to do? She would have to get away from him. Maybe she would go and visit her sister. Or maybe she would just cash in her savings and fly to some obscure island in the back of beyond.

'You're hurting me,' she whispered, and his lips twisted into a cold, sneering smile.

'Am I? I do apologise.' But he didn't slacken his hold on her.

'I'm not your property,' she flared, with a renewal of anger. 'I resent your treating me as though I am! You have no right to follow me here! I could have you arrested!'

'On what charges?' he inquired silkily. 'Don't be utterly ridiculous.'

'I'll call the police and have you thrown out!' she warned and he looked at her as though she had suddenly turned senile.

'Don't you know that the police aren't that keen on sticking their noses into lovers' tiffs?'

'I am not your lover!'

His eyes darkened and she knew with cold dread before his lips actually met hers that he was going to kiss her. She could see the intent in his eyes, but not the savagery with which he would do it. His mouth covered hers with swift, fierce hunger, prising her lips open so that she could scarcely breathe against him. Her head flew back under the impact of his kiss and as she struggled against him she could feel his fingers tighten on her arms, only relinquishing their grip to move to her back. He pulled her against him, their bodies so close that she could feel him hard and aroused against her.

And God, was she aroused. When she should be furious, her body was reacting in all the wrong ways. It was melting, wanting to yield to his power. She wanted to close her eyes and allow herself to be swept away on the tide of passion flowing through her.

His hand moved to cup her breast and he groaned into her mouth. She wasn't wearing a bra and his fingers found her nipple, rubbing it until it throbbed to feel the moistness of his mouth. He feverishly pushed up her blouse and she shuddered as his flesh made contact with hers. It was only when she felt his fingers urgently begin to explore her underneath her lacy underwear that sanity reasserted itself like a cruel slap across the face.

What had she been thinking of? She opened her eyes, horrified at her lack of control, at the ease with which she had abandoned common sense, and with a sudden movement pushed him hard.

He was not expecting that. She looked at his face and realised that he was still dazed with desire. It should have given her a rush of power, to know that she could arouse him to this pitch, but then she thought of the jet-haired woman who had shared his table at the restaurant. Was he like this in her arms? Would he retire to her house and finish what she, Natalie, was unable to?

The thought brought on a swift attack of self-disgust. 'I hope you're satisfied!' she said violently. 'You're not content to just force your way into my flat—oh, no, you have to force your way with me as well! What are you trying to prove? That you're bigger and stronger than me?'

He reached out and curled his fist into a handful of her hair. 'What I'm trying to prove, my witch, is that you can't marry that man!' He was back in full command of himself now. Only the slight huskiness in his voice suggested his lack of control a minute ago.

Natalie wished that she could take command of her senses with equal speed. Her body was still trembling from his lovemaking. It took a few seconds for his words to sink in, and when they did she looked at him in surprise.

'What are you talking about?' she asked.

'Don't pretend you don't know,' Kane rasped. 'I bounced into that man outside your flat and he was obviously in high humour. He couldn't wait to inform me that he was getting married.'

Comprehension dawned on Natalie's face. Eric had, she admitted, been walking on cloud nine all evening. He had probably volunteered the information without prompting, but had omitted to mention the woman to whom he was being married. Anna was, after all, Kane's ex-lover. Maybe Eric thought that if he mentioned any names he would be at the receiving-end of Kane's wrath.

The thought brought a reluctant smile to her lips.

'I'm glad you find it amusing,' he shot at her. 'How can you debase yourself by agreeing to marry a man you don't love and are very probably not attracted to?'

'And who said that I'm not attracted to Eric?' Natalie asked, avoiding his direct question.

'The way that you're attracted to me? You can't marry him. I won't allow it.'

'*You* won't allow it? I had no idea that the rest of the world needed permission from you to get married!'

'They don't. Only you.' The thick possessiveness in his voice made her pulses race, but this time she wasn't going to be taken in by him. His possessiveness had nothing to do with love.

'You can't stop me from doing what I want,' Natalie replied ambiguously. 'There was never anything between us. Not really.' She crossed her fingers behind her back. 'It's time for us both to lead our own lives now. I don't tell you what you should do with your personal life, do I?' Bitterness crept into her tone. 'You come here, ranting and raving, trying to lay the law down with me, but I don't exactly see you refraining from consoling yourself elsewhere.'

There was a definite glint in his eyes now when he looked at her.

'Are you jealous?' he asked, and she realised that he would love that.

She shook her head and made her face go blank. 'No, I'm not.'

Kane's lips tightened and he said roughly, 'There's a difference between having dinner with someone and agreeing to marry them. I'm thinking of you,' he said craftily. 'You'd end up miserable if you tied yourself with someone like Eric. I've told you this in the past, but I'm saying it again. You're a fool to try and make happiness out of whatever you have with that boy.'

'So you're thinking about me,' Natalie mocked. 'How altruistic.' At that, he had the grace to blush and she thought, You cad; talk about using every trick in the book. Unfinished business. That was what she was to him. Passion severed in mid-stream. No doubt if she had let it all run its course he would have tired of her soon enough and she would have been discarded to carry on with her own life. She knew him like the back of her hand. And if she hadn't been so deeply emotionally involved with him maybe she would have enjoyed the physical temptations he was offering without any fuss at all.

'Don't marry him,' he said roughly. 'At least if you marry me we would have great sex.'

That made her turn away, hurt. It was all he associated with a relationship, wasn't it?

'Get out of my flat,' she said, moving towards the door and pulling it open. Kane shot her a look that implied that he would have loved to shake her until she came round to his way of thinking, but he didn't say anything.

Outside, the deserted street reminded her how late it was. Well past midnight. She would be a wreck in the morning. She was finding it difficult enough to wake up in time for work without having had only a few hour's sleep the night before.

His car was parked across the street, under one of the streetlamps, sleek and sharp, a bit like its owner. She wondered what had happened to his date. Had he packed her off in a taxi back to her house? Or maybe she was waiting back at his. The thought made her want to retch and she looked at him with cool resentment.

'You're a stupid fool,' he informed her and she bristled angrily.

'Then I can't imagine what you're doing here,' she retorted. 'It's not your scene to keep company with stupid fools, is it?'

He looked as if he could hit her for that remark. In the shadows, his face was all angles, hard and uncompromising, and she wondered how on earth she could ever have had the temerity to fall in love with him.

'Fine. Throw your life away. I'll leave you to get on with it.' He turned and walked away, his footsteps ringing on the deserted pavement. She watched, unable to tear her eyes away, until he let himself into the car and slammed the door shut behind him. She knew that he wasn't looking at her. He had washed his hands of her. He pulled out smoothly and the car vanished into the distance, but instead of feeling relief Natalie could only muster up a feeling of loss.

She slept badly and awoke to a feeling of nausea. She had not suffered from severe morning sickness with her pregnancy—more a vague feeling of nausea that lasted on and off for the entire day—but this morning she felt positively ill.

She was ashen when she finally made it into work and Tony glanced briefly at her as she entered, concerned at her pallor, but he soon forgot about it when the usual round of phone calls and meetings rushed him off his feet.

What a wonderful boss, Natalie thought; she could just get on with her work and her nausea without him hovering around her like a mother hen.

She thought of Kane. Nothing like a mother hen, more like a predatory eagle, but nevertheless if she had shown up for work feeling as she did those shrewd eyes of his would have spotted it instantly and he would not have let the matter rest until he had dragged the truth out of her. Persistence was a trait with which he had been abundantly supplied.

She sat at her desk, automatically sifting through her post, but her mind was fluttering back to the time when she worked with Kane. He had been demanding, forceful, keeping her on her toes every second that she was in the office, but she had loved it. He had fired her adrenalin so that each evening she had returned to her flat with a feeling of having achieved something. Working for Tony was nice, but he operated on a different scale altogether. She would, she reflected, miss him more than she would miss the surroundings or the work.

On the Wednesday, Eric phoned, excited, to inform her that he was going to be married on the Friday afternoon and would she be able to make it.

'This Friday?' Natalie asked, stunned at the speed with which his love life had recently progressed. 'Isn't that a bit soon? I thought you said next week.'

'I know I've only known her a short time...'

'But it's the real thing?' She laughed, hoping that he would not live to see his optimism misplaced. It was one thing rushing off into marriage with someone you were desperately in love with, but time could wreak havoc with one's illusions. She was fond of Eric. She hoped that he was doing the right thing, but there was no way that she would dream of lecturing to him about his decision.

'You and Claire will be the only people there,' he told her. 'My parents are out of the country, though from

the sound of their reception to the news I seriously doubt
that they would have seen fit to attend.'

'I'm sure you're wrong,' Natalie said.

'You always were an optimist.'

Natalie patted her stomach unconsciously with an
ironic half-smile. 'Realist. Some situations you can't
change. You just have to make the best of them. What
time on Friday?' she asked, changing the subject, and
they chatted for a while about the details.

Natalie would have loved to speak to Anna, to see
exactly how bowled over she was with Eric; after all, she
had been quite taken with Kane, and Kane and Eric were
hardly similar types. Curiosity, she thought, killed the
cat. What if the answer to that isn't what I want to hear?
Anna might well see Eric as no more than a reliable meal
ticket after the stimulating but insecure rollercoaster ride
with Kane. A timely and convenient revenge. She hoped
not.

A sudden blitz of phone calls snapped her out of her
train of thought, and for the remainder of the day she
found herself struggling to do not only her own
workload, but also that of the only other secretary who
had taken the day off sick.

She completely forgot to mention Friday to Tony, to
tell him that she would be taking the time off work to
go to the register office. It was only on Friday morning
that she remembered her oversight, and she waited
anxiously for him to appear through the door. Which
he did, about half an hour before she was due to leave.

Natalie stood up abruptly when she saw him, and said,
'Tony. I have to ask a favour of you. Is it all right if I
leave work early this afternoon? In fact, in about twenty
minutes' time?'

Tony looked at her, dismayed. 'What about work?' he asked. 'Susie's still not in!'

'I'm more or less up to date with the important stuff,' Natalie informed him. 'But if you like I'll take some work home with me.'

He shook his head and smiled at her. 'No need. You've been working hard. You deserve the time off. My wife says that I'm becoming an ogre. Work, work, work and not much else.' The telephone rang and he picked it up, and Natalie collected her bag and jacket. When he finished talking, he looked at her more closely. 'Now that you mention it, you do look dressier than usual. Where are you off to?'

She told him the name of the register office, glancing at her watch and realising that she would have to get her skates on if she was going to be there on time.

'Register office?' Tony followed her out to the door, his forehead creased into a frown.

'Yes.' Natalie looked at him breathlessly and said apologetically, 'And I'm sorry I gave you such short notice, but you know how it is. It was a spur-of-the-moment decision on Eric's part.'

She smiled briefly and thought of Eric, the least likely person in the world she would have associated with spur-of-the-moment decisions, which only went to prove how love could make the average person act completely out of character.

Tony was nodding. 'Well, my dear, all the best.'

Natalie gave him a vague smile and mumbled something about passing it on to Eric, but her thoughts were already flying off to what Underground train she would need to catch and whether she should simply grab a taxi instead outside the office, and spare herself the trauma of taking the Tube.

In the end, she caught a taxi and spent just as long sitting in traffic as if she had caught the connecting Tube trains to her destination.

Eric was waiting outside, his eyes darting from the watch to the road. Anna, it transpired, had not yet arrived, and he laughed nervously at Natalie.

'I'd hate to become a statistic.'

'Statistic?' Claire was running up the steps where her taxi had deposited her, and Natalie waved in her friend's direction.

'One of those men who get stood up at the altar.'

'You won't be,' Natalie reassured him. 'And, besides, there won't be an altar.'

'Well, then,' Eric said drily, 'I suppose that's something to be grateful for.'

Claire bounded up to them, her face flushed from the exertion of running, and hugged Natalie enthusiastically.

'You haven't called me in over a fortnight,' she accused, and Natalie shot her a guilty look.

'I haven't been very sociable recently,' she admitted. 'In fact, I think I've forgotten where the phone in the flat is.'

Claire giggled uncontrollably at that while Eric worriedly scoured the street for approaching taxis, in between nervously adjusting his tie.

'Don't worry,' Natalie whispered, 'she'll be here. She's only fifteen minutes late. Have you met her?' She turned to Claire who shook her head.

'Actually, I've been rather busy myself. Out of the country for ten days. I'm only just getting back into the swing of things over here.'

Just then, Eric muttered under his breath, 'At long last,' and both women turned to see Anna moving unhurriedly towards them while Eric gesticulated at his watch frantically.

Claire's mouth dropped open and Natalie whispered to her, 'I think your jaws will become unhinged if you don't close your mouth soon.'

Claire's teeth snapped together. 'Is that her?'

Eric was hurrying down to kiss Anna, a look of rapture on his face, and Natalie nodded drily. 'Does she live up to your expectations?'

'Wow! What does she see in my brother? Wasn't she involved with your ex-boss? Correct me if I'm wrong, but he was way out of Eric's league, wasn't he?'

Natalie tensed. Even talking about Kane had the ability to make her feel flustered and defensive, even when that talk was only casual conversation. His image might subside occasionally but it was always there, waiting to pop out against her will.

'You're right,' Natalie answered, her voice a shade cooler, 'he wasn't in Eric's league, by which I mean that Eric was way ahead of him in every respect.'

Claire tore her eyes away from Anna, now swaying up the steps on Eric's arm, and looked at Natalie with interest.

'Do I detect a note of bitterness there?'

'Of course not,' Natalie said hurriedly, 'just stating facts.' She moved down, curious to see how Anna would respond to her, and much as she expected the other woman looked at her with a mixture of embarrassment and defensiveness.

'Eric didn't tell me that you would be here,' she said petulantly, her fingers tightening on his arm, and Eric looked delighted at this small show of jealous pique.

'I'll try not to be obvious,' Natalie said obligingly, and got a scowl for her efforts.

They trooped quickly up to the building and after a few minutes of scouring signs managed to locate the general direction of the register office.

It was a room. One room with some seats. They were shown in and told to wait, and Natalie looked around her curiously. Eric and Anna were talking under their breath, but even so their voices rebounded against the walls, reminding them how empty of people the place was.

Not romantic, but that didn't seem to bother either Eric or Anna overmuch. He was staring at her, besotted, and she, Natalie noticed, was responding with sheer delight. Adoration had its own peculiar sex appeal, and Anna was basking in Eric's adoration. Natalie looked at the two of them with envy and a vague feeling of longing. I'll never find anyone, she thought. There won't be anyone there for me or for my baby.

Eric glanced across at her and then walked towards her, while Claire meandered off to chat to Anna, making theatrical noises about really having to get to know her sister-in-law-to-be.

'Where's this registrar?' Eric asked Natalie in a peevish tone. 'He's late. Twenty minutes late.'

Natalie looked vaguely at the door and shrugged her shoulders. 'Maybe,' she said with a stab at humour, 'he's got pre-wedding nerves.'

Eric wasn't paying her the slightest bit of attention. His eyes were fixed on the door as if he was willing it to open.

'Besides,' Natalie sounded, 'it's a chance for Claire to chat to Anna a bit before you two tie the knot.'

Eric turned to look at his sister and his wife-to-be who were standing towards the back of the room and he grunted something about supposing so. All the same,

Natalie could understand his anxiety to get it all over and done with. She didn't exactly relish the thought of standing around in the room for an indefinite length of time either. She wanted to get back to her flat. Not that she had anything planned. Recently, she seemed to be cultivating inactivity, even though she knew that it was not a healthy lifestyle.

She opened her mouth to chat in platitudes to Eric, anything to put a stop to that awful nervous tension that seemed to be overwhelming him, when the door was pushed open. Hard. It banged back against the wall, and Eric said, 'Thank God. Here at last,' even though he looked faintly startled. Natalie had a polite smile plastered on her face, and she reassuringly squeezed Eric's arm.

But it wasn't the registrar. What registrar, she asked herself afterwards, went around banging doors?

It was Kane, and he definitely did not look as though he had come to wish the happy couple all the best.

CHAPTER TEN

ALL four stopped talking and stared at Kane in shocked amazement. It didn't take much imagination to know how they looked—like four people who had personally seen Banquo's ghost. It would have been comical, but Natalie didn't feel much like laughing at all. She stared at Kane's face while her mind desperately tried to work out what he was doing here.

Eric was the first to break the silence. He laughed nervously and said in quite a controlled voice, considering the unexpected nature of the situation, 'I thought you were the registrar.' He cleared his throat and approached Kane to shake his hand. 'He's running a bit late.' He held out his hand to Kane who looked at it as if it were something quite repellant and most probably contagious, and Eric's face flushed with bewilderment and then anger. 'What are you doing here anyway?' he asked in a more aggressive tone. 'I don't recall having asked you.' He shot a look towards Anna who was still stiff with shock.

'You didn't,' Kane said grimly, his eyes raking over Natalie. He walked across to her, unhurriedly, and said in a disturbingly polite voice, 'And after all the years we spent together I would have thought that an invitation was the least I could expect.' He obviously had not noticed Anna hovering in the background, or if he had he had chosen to ignore her.

Either way, Natalie still couldn't work out his presence here. She frowned, puzzled, and he looked at her sar-

donically, as if to say, Please spare me the butter-
wouldn't-melt-in-mouth routine.

'You don't know Eric,' she pointed out automatically.
'How did you find out that we would be here anyway?'

He wasn't looking at anyone else in the room at all
by this point. His eyes were fixed on Natalie's face and
she was finding it hard to meet his stare levelly and
calmly.

'I phoned your boss. He told me where you were.'

'Oh.' She looked across to Eric and lifted her shoulders
in a slight shrug and the gesture seemed to enrage Kane.

Claire hadn't said a word so far, nor had Anna. They
both appeared to have been struck dumb and Natalie
could well understand the reaction. She herself was
having some difficulty in getting the words out.

None of them heard the door being pushed open until
the registrar spoke, his voice sharp into the tense silence.

'Am I in the right room?' he asked sternly, and Eric
nodded and began speaking with overdone enthusiasm.
He was clearly relieved to have someone else on the scene.
He was shaking the registrar's hand vigorously. At any
minute, Natalie thought, he'll embrace the poor man,
who obviously didn't have a clue as to what was going
on.

'Well, I'm running behind schedule,' he said to
everyone at large, extracting his hand from Eric's and
placing it safely behind his back. He took his place
behind the desk in the front of the room and slipped on
a pair of glasses. 'I do apologise for the delay, but are
we all ready now?'

He didn't look up. These things always went ac-
cording to plan, no doubt. His words were just a for-
mality. He hardly expected an interruption. None of
them did.

Natalie was still looking at Kane out of the corner of her eyes, but she was quite prepared to let the ceremony take place, and then try and figure out what was going on here with him. She looked directly ahead of her, at the registrar's downbent head. It would be extremely short, she knew. There would be no long sermon or elaborate blessings, just the few simple words necessary to marrying two people. They began to move into their positions, when Kane spoke, his voice harsh.

'There is not going to be a marriage.'

All four froze and the registrar looked up, startled. Natalie had an insane desire to burst out laughing, which she controlled by looking down at her feet and keeping a perfectly straight face.

'I beg your pardon, young man?' the registrar said, shocked. He looked around at the gathering of people and said sharply, 'Is this some kind of joke?'

'No, sir.' Eric moved towards the registrar, placating, while he glared sideways at Kane with hatred. 'I have no idea what this man is doing here, sir. I barely know him.'

Out of the five of them, Kane appeared to be the only one still in control. He had folded his arms across his chest, and Natalie could feel his eyes boring into her, willing her to look up, something which she had no intention of doing.

'Would someone mind explaining just what is going on here?' the registrar asked. 'I'm a busy man. I don't have time for these sorts of games.'

'No games.' Kane moved forward. 'There is to be no marriage.'

For the first time since Kane's entrance, Anna stepped forward and spoke, her voice hard. 'Kane, what the hell is going on?'

Kane threw her a disdainful look. 'A witness, Anna? I had no idea you were that friendly with Natalie.'

'I'm not,' Anna said, and in a flash Natalie understood what was going on. It should have been obvious from the very start, but things had happened so quickly and so unexpectedly that her brain had hardly had time to put two and two together.

Kane had said that he had found out where she was from Tony. Dear, vague Tony. Had he thought that she and Eric were about to tie the knot? He must have, and this must have been the message he had conveyed to Kane.

So why, she asked herself with an excitement which she tried to staunch, had he rushed over here?

'I think you've made a mistake,' she said softly, turning to Kane, and he glared at her.

'I think you are the one who has made the mistake,' he said harshly. He moved towards her, taking her elbow in his hand, but before he could elaborate Natalie said quickly,

'I'm not getting married. Not that it would have been any of your business if I had been. No, I'm not marrying Eric.' Her eyes flitted across to Anna. 'Anna is.'

It didn't take Kane long to catch on that he had made a mistake on a huge scale. A split second, in fact. By this time, Anna had approached the desk by Eric and had linked her hand defensively through his arm. She really loves him, Natalie thought, before her attention once more refocused on the man looming over her.

'You could have told me from the start,' Kane muttered under his breath, 'and spared us all this scene.' He looked so utterly sheepish that Natalie smiled, and he threw her an accusing frown. 'Everything's been sorted out,' he said with a calmness that she could only admire. 'Please do carry on.'

'Are you sure?' The registrar looked around his little audience. 'No more surprises?' He glanced at Claire. 'Surely an outburst is due from your corner?'

Claire grinned, her composure back in place. 'None that I can think of, sir.'

The registrar mumbled something under his breath that didn't sound terribly amused, and then launched into his little speech, which he knew off pat.

As far as Natalie was concerned, it all went in one ear and out of the other. She was simply far too aware of Kane's presence next to her to pay any attention to what the registrar was saying. He could have been casting spells and she would not have been any the wiser. Did she mean so much to Kane that he would actually have put a stop to her marrying Eric, if that was what she had intended to do?

No, she told herself rationally. He just would not see anything so terribly wrong in doing it because he was convinced that she felt nothing for Eric, and the reason that he felt that way was because he knew the power that he himself had over her.

So don't start over-reacting, she thought, and just remember that you will never be free to do anything with him anyway, because there's the baby. Mistakes are made to be learnt from, and there's nothing romantic about his gesture. At bottom, it's probably just selfish after all.

As soon as the short service was over, he hustled her out of the room, ignoring Eric's piqued question to Natalie as to whether she had forgotten that they were all going to have a bite to eat. Natalie looked over her shoulder helplessly. 'I'll join you later,' she said with a miserable attempt at an apologetic smile, and Kane growled.

'I wouldn't bank on it.'

As soon as the door was shut behind him, she wriggled against his grip, finally giving up, and said in a high voice, 'You can't do this.'

'No?' Kane said softly. 'And who exactly is going to stop me?'

'I'll scream,' she threatened, and he raised his eyebrows.

'No, you won't,' he said calmly, leading her out into the sunshine. 'You're far too curious to find out what all that was about.'

Natalie hated to admit it, but he was right. She had no intention of screaming. She allowed herself to be led to where his car had been parked on double yellow lines, and she sat in silence as he pulled away from the kerb, away from the centre of the city.

'Where are you taking me?' she asked, and before he could answer she added sarcastically, 'I don't suppose it would do any good telling you that I just want to get back to work.'

'You suppose right.' His hands were resting loosely on the steering-wheel, and even though his voice was composed enough there was an element there that she couldn't quite recognise and had never heard before. Or maybe it was just her imagination playing tricks on her.

'How many more times do I have to tell you to leave me alone?' she asked, and he didn't answer. There was an air of tension about him, even though he seemed re-laxed enough.

The car cruised out of London, on to the M4, where it picked up speed on the motorway. Natalie looked at the vanishing and comforting crowds of the city with dismay. Where on earth were they heading?

'Windsor,' he said, reading her mind and glancing across to her. 'We need to talk.'

'Why did you barge into the register office?'

'That's one of the things we need to talk about.' His profile was hard and clean, and she couldn't glean a thing from it. He only ever revealed what he wanted to be seen, and right now it was very little.

She turned to stare out of the window. Outside the scenery, not particularly charming, flashed past her, and she was only aware that they had reached Windsor when the car turned off the motorway and skilfully manoeuvred the small, picturesque streets, dominated by the castle looming over the town like a benevolent patriarch.

He was, she realised, as involved with his thoughts as she was, and she didn't know whether that made her feel any better or not.

The car pulled up outside a restaurant on the outskirts of the city centre—one of those old-fashioned places which had probably achieved its look through a clever combination of skill and attention to the right sort of detail. It was crowded with a clientele of businessmen, but Kane was recognised instantly. Instead of being shown into the main restaurant, they were taken up the stairs to a sitting-room.

'I know the owner personally. This is his retreat from the madhouse downstairs.'

Natalie didn't reply. She didn't want to start on a long, polite conversation. There were too many questions screaming for answers in her head. She sat down on one of the comfortable flowered sofas and tucked her legs underneath her. Kane's green eyes flicked over her, making her uncomfortable, and she thought that he was going to say something but he didn't. He stood up and prowled around the sitting-room, inspecting the pictures on the walls as though they were masterpieces instead of pleasant enough prints, moving to stare out of the window.

At last, he said heavily, not looking at her, 'I suppose you think my behaviour was laughable?'

Did he really expect an answer to that one? Natalie wondered. But she couldn't summon up any antagonism towards him, though she knew that that was her best defence. His defensive, aggressive tone somehow made him achingly vulnerable.

'We were all surprised,' she said neutrally.

'And you don't think that I was as well?'

Natalie could feel her heart hammering away inside of her, and her thoughts were sluggish. Explain yourself! she wanted to shout. Don't play games with me.

He moved around to where she was sitting and her body tensed. If he lays a finger on me, she promised herself, I'll fly out of here before he can so much as move a muscle. She eyed the door, assessing the distance, and he followed the line of her stare.

'Forget it,' he said in a low voice. 'You seem to have been running away from me forever, but now it's time to stop.' Natalie sprang up, alarmed and frightened by something on his face, and he pushed her back down on to the sofa.

'I'm not afraid of you,' she bit out, 'and you can keep me prisoner here till the cows come home, but it won't get you anywhere. I'm not going to sleep with you.'

'Whatever gave you the idea that that was what I brought you here for?'

Her temple began to throb and she couldn't prevent
the little flutter of hope that sprang up inside of her.
One tiny drop of water, she thought bitterly, and the
seed will grow, but let's not forget that that drop of water
won't keep it alive for very long.

He sat on the edge of the coffee-table in front of her,
barring her exit, and Natalie stared at him with defiance.

'Don't look at me like that, woman,' he muttered,
'I'm not going to devour you.'

'This is all a waste of time,' she whispered, looking
down at her hands.

He reached out and lifted her chin with one finger,
and she felt as though she was drowning in the green
pools of his eyes.

'You let me think that you and Eric were an ongoing
thing,' he said accusingly.

'What difference did it make?' Her voice sounded
cracked and strained, but still proud.

'Dammit, Natalie, can't you see what you're doing to
me?' He raked one restless hand through his thick black
hair and she followed the gesture with compelling absorption. 'Do you want me to beg?' he asked, looking
away.

'No. I would hate that.'

'I'll beg if it means the difference between you going
or staying,' he said in such a low voice that she found
it difficult to understand the words.

'I can't stay as your mistress,' Natalie said, but she
was confused. She wanted him so badly, loved him so
badly, that next to that everything else seemed to fade
into insignificance.

Oh, God, she thought suddenly, how could I have forgotten the baby?

'Marry me,' he whispered, his voice uneven. 'I've asked you to before. Marry me, please. I'm begging.'

Tell me that you love me, she willed him to say, and their eyes met.

'You know I do, don't you?' The smile he gave her was crooked. She could hardly believe her ears. She seemed to have spent a lifetime waiting for these words, but now that they were spoken she wondered whether she had heard correctly. Maybe she had misinterpreted him.

'I love you, Natalie,' he said with a wrenched sigh, and her body began to tremble uncontrollably. 'I never thought that I'd hear myself say those words. I always imagined that love was something I could control, that I'd be able to beckon it when I wanted it, when it suited me, but life has a funny way of kicking your best laid plans on the head, doesn't it?'

'Doesn't it?'

He reached out and stroked the sensitive skin on her wrist with his thumb and the rhythmic warmth made her groan slightly.

'You excite me,' he said softly. 'You're exciting me now, and I don't think that this is quite the place, do you? At least, not with the door unlocked.' He stood up and walked across to the door, clicking the lock into place, then he returned to sit next to her.

'I went crazy when I thought that you were getting married to that man,' Kane told her, his hand cupping the side of her face, then moving down to caress her neck and shoulders. 'What did you tell Tony, for God's sake?'

Natalie smiled. 'I told him that I was going to the register office. He must have misinterpreted what I meant.'

'His mistake put me through hell.' He leant forward and brushed his lips against hers, then his kiss deepened into one of fierce hunger. Natalie fell back under his onslaught. She was breathing quickly, feeling that rushing, heady excitement that only he could arouse in her. 'I love you, darling,' he moaned, and when he lifted his head to look at her his eyes were feverish and sensual. 'Tell me that you love me.'

'You know I do,' she said softly, tracing her finger along his jaw. 'I've loved you for years. I can't imagine how you could ever have thought that there was anything between Eric and me. It would have been convenient—after all, I never imagined that you could be interested in me—but love doesn't listen to reason, does it?' She paused and looked at him anxiously. 'There's something else,' she said hesitantly.

'Mmm?' Kane murmured, one hand reaching out to cup her breast while his finger found her nipple and teased it into sweet arousal.

'You're making it very hard for me to concentrate,' she said shakily. Her body was aching for him. She could hardly think straight.

'Good,' he said, undoing the buttons of her blouse and staring with concentrated hunger at her exposed breast. 'Now you know how I've been feeling recently. All those years, you worked your way under my skin. Do you know, I thought about you all the time when I was in the Far East? I told myself that I was only drawing comparisons between you and the secretary that I had out there, but deep down I knew that I was missing you for completely different reasons.'

His hand stroked her thighs under the fine linen of her skirt, hitching it up so that he could find the tender moistness waiting for his touch.

'But I was fat then,' Natalie said, momentarily distracted, and he laughed softly.

'You don't believe that love has anything to do with looks, do you? What a chauvinistic remark from a woman.'

'The women you dated were always so beautiful,' Natalie protested, blushing. His words pierced her with a sweet sense of satisfaction. Had he really noticed her? She thought back to the odd times she had caught him looking at her from under his lashes, holding her stare for just a fraction more than was necessary. She had never paid the slightest bit of attention to it. She had never felt that she possessed what it took for a man like Kane Marshall to find her attractive. Her own insecurity had blinded her.

'I didn't fall in love with any of them,' he pointed out, and she smiled, then she shot him a quick, uncertain look.

'There's just one thing,' she said hesitantly, 'one very big thing.'

'What?' His tone was dry. 'You've made me admit that I'm head over heels in love with you, I actually made a complete fool of myself at that damned register office just to prove it. I've begged you for your hand in marriage. What else? Do I have to have it written in the sky?'

'That sounds a novel idea.' But her eyes when she looked at him were still serious.

'We love each other, my darling. What more could there possibly be?'

Natalie thought about what she was going to say. A man who happily contemplated marriage didn't automatically contemplate fatherhood with the same enthusiasm. What if he was not ready for that final step?

She tried to think back to everything he had ever said about family life, about wanting a family, but her mind went blank, and all she could think of was the fact that he loved her.

'I didn't mean for it to happen,' she said huskily, and he frowned, looking at her as if trying to fathom out what she was telling him, and already suspecting the worst.

'Mean for what to happen?' he said slowly.

Natalie rested her hand on her stomach and he followed her movement. She could see recognition dawning in his eyes, though when he raised his head to stare at her there was enough of a question there to make her nod her head in confirmation.

'I'm pregnant.'

'And you didn't tell me?' he said roughly, but his eyes were hot and possessive, making her skin burn.

'I didn't want to... to make you feel that you had any responsibilities towards me. As far as I was concerned, you didn't love me, and I thought that my pregnancy would only force you into a corner.' She laughed drily. 'In all the time I've known you, the one thing you've always made clear is the fact that you hate a woman who tries to force you into a corner.'

'You little fool,' he broke out, but he was trembling slightly as his mouth covered hers in a tender kiss. He stroked her breasts, then her stomach, and she could feel the wonder in his touch.

'You don't mind?' she asked stupidly and he raised dazed eyes to hers.

'Mind? I would have killed you if you had run away from me with my baby inside you. I should be as angry as hell, but I can understand how you must have felt.' Under her skirt, his hand found the bare flesh of her stomach, and he caressed her gently. 'Fatherhood *and* marriage. If anyone had told me a year ago that that would have been my destiny, and that I would have wanted it more than I've wanted anything in my life, I would have laughed in their face. No, I would have run to the opposite end of the earth.' His fingers found the swell of her breast and he caressed it with soft movements that made her want to cry out in desire.

'I'll never stop you if that's want you want to do.'

'I hope you don't mean that, because I would damn well lock you up if *you* ever tried to get away from me.' He laughed, and buried his face in her neck.

Natalie sighed and lay back on the sofa, her fingers curling in his hair.

'Can we do this?' he asked uncertainly.

'Do what?' she asked innocently. 'I didn't realise that we were doing anything.'

'Didn't you?' he growled, possessing her mouth fiercely. 'You little witch.'

She laughed contentedly. 'I may be pregnant, but I'm not a piece of china. And I want you, Kane Marshall. I'll never stop wanting you.'

'Good,' he murmured with satisfaction. 'Because now that you've got me you'll never be able to let me go.'

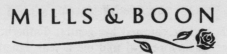

Proudly present
to you...

BETTY NEELS' 100TH ROMANCE

Betty has been writing for Mills & Boon
Romances for over 20 years. She began
once she had retired from her job as a Ward
Sister. She is married to a Dutchman and
spent many years in Holland. Both her
experiences as a nurse and her knowledge
and love of Holland feature in many of her
novels.

Her latest romance *'AT ODDS WITH LOVE'*
is available from August 1993, price £1.80.

Next Month's Romances

Each month you can choose from a wide variety of romance with Mills & Boon. Below are the new titles to look out for next month, why not ask either Mills & Boon Reader Service or your Newsagent to reserve you a copy of the titles you want to buy – just tick the titles you would like and either post to Reader Service or take it to any Newsagent and ask them to order your books.

Please save me the following titles:		Please tick √
THE WEDDING	Emma Darcy	
LOVE WITHOUT REASON	Alison Fraser	
FIRE IN THE BLOOD	Charlotte Lamb	
GIVE A MAN A BAD NAME	Roberta Leigh	
TRAVELLING LIGHT	Sandra Field	
A HEALING FIRE	Patricia Wilson	
AN OLD ENCHANTMENT	Amanda Browning	
STRANGERS BY DAY	Vanessa Grant	
CONSPIRACY OF LOVE	Stephanie Howard	
FIERY ATTRACTION	Emma Richmond	
RESCUED	Rachel Elliot	
DEFIANT LOVE	Jessica Hart	
BOGUS BRIDE	Elizabeth Duke	
ONE SHINING SUMMER	Quinn Wilder	
TRUST TOO MUCH	Jayne Bauling	
A TRUE MARRIAGE	Lucy Gordon	

If you would like to order these books in addition to your regular subscription from Mills & Boon Reader Service please send £1.80 per title to: Mills & Boon Reader Service, Freepost, P.O. Box 236, Croydon, Surrey, CR9 9EL, quote your Subscriber No:.................................... (If applicable) and complete the name and address details below. Alternatively, these books are available from many local Newsagents including W.H.Smith, J.Menzies, Martins and other paperback stockists from 10 September 1993.

Name:...

Address:...

....Post Code:........................

To Retailer: If you would like to stock M&B books please contact your regular book/magazine wholesaler for details.

You may be mailed with offers from other reputable companies as a result of this application. If you would rather not take advantage of these opportunities please tick box ☐